Toxic

Passion

LaKymbria Rhodes

DEDICATION

To the soft girl who loves passionately with her whole heart, the girl who fights hard for who she loves, the girl who plans to leave, but just can't see life beyond leaving the person you put your whole heart into, the girl who finally got sick and tired and did what she had to do, the girl who chose peace, the girl who is healing, the girl with unique perspectives and who is often misunderstood, and to the friends, family and genuine supporters of these girls, this is for you!!!

CONTENTS

ACKNOWLEDGMENTS

Thank you to everyone who has loved, respected and accepted me
unconditionally.
Thank you for seeing me.
Thank you for encouraging me.
Thank you for pushing me.
Thank you for supporting me.
Book Cover Photoshoot by Chad Lawson
Edited by Kathy Hardison

Prelude

The year was 2020. You can remember the year Kobe died, Covid 19 hit the U.S and created a global pandemic, more black lives were taken, and rioters protested in full force. Every time we blinked our eyes, we were haunted by another shocking but not surprising news story or post. Although many were quarantined, in a constant panic, and unemployed, there was one mother fucker who saw these times to be the perfect alignment for his mission – Cupid.

I know what you are thinking, "how sweet, another love story." It is a love story, but take everything you think you know about love out of your brain and extend your mental capabilities beyond its capacity and allow your eyes to see visions that you can never imagine. Thank me later for warning you. I, however, was not given that disclaimer. I did not have the option not to have my soul abruptly snatched from me and placed in the softest hands and warmest arms a human can ever possess.

What do I mean by not having the option? I mean even with the strongest guards I secured over my heart while burying it in the deepest chamber of my soul, making it pretty damn near impossible to let anyone in, she, yes, she pierced through all of it and literally snatched my soul from me and somehow intertwined it with hers. What's even crazier is that it didn't feel as remotely close to how I metaphorically described it to be. It felt wanted. It felt aligned. It felt genuine.

It didn't help that our sexual desires for each other were ultimately high. Her touch spoke directly to my love language, without my ever saying a word. Almost everything about her was me, and everything about me was her. Our energy radiated and attracted so many people to us no matter where we were.

This connection, unlike anything I have felt before, was just different. Like, damn, if you know something is mutually there, just cut to the chase and be together. Right? Wrong! See, even the universe

4

couldn't align all the stars in our favor. The angels in heaven couldn't just grace us with each other. We had opposing forces. They were obvious. They were morally reasonable. They made circumstances extremely difficult. The kind of difficulty that keeps the mind, body, and heart wrestling against each other. All rightfully serving their own purpose while at the same time fighting to see which one will solely determine the fate of this toxic yet passionate twin flame. Coincidently, her name was Skyy, and mine, Starr.

1 Impressions

It was the morning of July 17th. I was opening the store where we worked. Just about a quarter to 7am, she walked in ready for her first day. She introduced herself and wanted to let someone know that she was on time for her shift. I was impressed with how she articulated herself and how punctual and professional she presented herself. I could also sense in this exact moment that she was about her money. I didn't feel anything at this particular time because my attention was being occupied by another person, but I did notice her presence.

I continued to observe how she thoroughly completed her work tasks and took the initiative to take on more responsibilities when her tasks were complete. Fast forward to one day when I finally decided to acknowledge her presence on another level and bypass the passersby stage. She was working on a task and had her lashes perfectly placed, giving her an extra glow this day. As soon as I gained enough courage, I opened my mouth with a slight gaze in my eyes and a flirtatious smile on my lips and asked, "Who did your lashes? They are very pretty."

She responded, "I did my own lashes and thank you."

Later that night, she told me she was leaving for a break and she would return. I jokingly, but somehow seriously, as I have learned this to be a skill of mine, responded, "Oh you must be going to smoke. I'm coming to smoke with you.

She laughed and said, "Ok come on."

At this point I believe she knew I was coming on to her and was very accepting of the energy I was putting out. I remember mentioning that I was heading out to the beach for a day and returning to work on Sunday. She asked if I were going to the beach with my girlfriends, referring to my platonic friends who were girls. All I heard was girlfriend and I immediately responded, "I don't have a girlfriend because these hoes not loyal." She gave me a smile that solidified a mutual understanding and acceptance for what we were both doing.

As the night of our shift together continued, she and I both made extra attempts to have contact with one another. It wasn't until we went outside to check the lot together, which meant clear the parking lot of all shopping carts she told me, "I got your front, your back, and your side" that I was assured of a mutual interest of some kind.

2 The arrangement

That Sunday I returned to work and Skyy was working too. We talked briefly about my beach trip and continued to converse. When I left that day, she walked me outside, and we both hinted that we wanted to talk some more. We hit each other with the, "Ok I'll talk to you later."

She was a little bolder than I and added, "Well how will we talk to each other later if we don't have each other's number?"

I smiled and responded, 'Well, get my number." She pulled out her phone and I started, "229..." She texted me her name and told me she was locking me in. I texted back, "Let me see." She screenshotted the message thread and my name was saved as "Little Baby." I replied with a laughing emoji and we continued with small talk.

We later exchanged pictures and shifted to a little more in depth conversation. I texted her, "What do you wish to be to me, and what do you want me to be in return?"

She texted back, "What titles are available?"

I responded, "My girlfriend, boo, or miscellaneous entangler."

She said, "I'll go with the last option."

I said, "Ok, bet." I tried to remember if I could recall her relationship status or if I ever knew it. We had a phone conversation not too long after we started texting. I asked her if she was single. Her response was, "Something like that."

I knew there was more explanation on what the hell that meant because in 2020, there is ALWAYS an explanation. So I replied, "Ok, meaning?"

She explained while referencing the interlocked female symbol tattoo on the left side of her neck with her ex-girlfriend's name, "I was with my ex-girlfriend for three years. She and I broke up, and I met my boyfriend, Solar. He knows I like girls, so he is fine with me having a girlfriend."

8

I remember thinking, ok this can be fun, but this can also be a little crazy. I know me, so I know if I catch feelings for her that I would at some point want her to myself and would probably want more than what she had to offer me. On the other hand, I could not be into her that much and could embrace the fun of this experience. Before I knew it, I looked up, and we had been on the phone for an hour. It's clear at this point I'm feeling shorty, and she's feeling me. I do not recall every detail in our first phone conversation, but I do remember a lot of laughing, detailed questions, and well thought out answers being exchanged.

As she tried to explain the agreement she and boyfriend had, I tried to understand it while helping her explain it to me. So I did ask, "Are you and he saying that the two of you are open to a polygamous relationship?"

She responded, "Polygamous relationship? No. That's not what it is." So instead of me trying to figure it all out in that given moment, I didn't. I knew the conversation would come up again at some point. We made plans to spend the upcoming weekend together. We agreed on a chill night and a night where we went out on the town for smoke, drinks, and good vibes.

Back to our plans to chill. We were very blunt that we wanted to fuck. Listen, we are two grown, sexy ass women! I wanted her and she was down with what I wanted. In fact, we anticipated hanging out the entire week. Our conversations mainly consisted of our upcoming plans as well as our dynamics. I noticed the more we tried to navigate our dynamics as far as placement in each other's lives the more difficult it became. It was like I was beginning to like something about her.

The next day, we texted and she reiterated that she comes as a package deal and how she only wanted to spice up her life with her boyfriend whom she loves. Although I understood we were only supposed to be fuck buddies, I couldn't grasp the idea of my fucking another nigga right now. I declined her offer, disappointed but confident that I made the right decision for myself. She continued to text stating that it was cool and that we could still hangout and move forward with our plans of getting to know each other as friends. I agreed and we continued to converse the rest of the day.

In my true fashion, I flirted every chance I could, and she reciprocated my energy. I should add that these conversations created and increased the sexual tension among us. Without my asking, Skyy sent me a video of her just saying hi and that she tried to take a cute pic but couldn't so she sent a video just for me.

I replied "LOL! How many people did you send this video to?"

She texted back, "It was just for you."

I asked "Are we going to have a sleepover when we hang out this weekend?"

She responded with a text that honestly shifted my mood. The texted stated, "That's too intimate. We're not in a relationship now." Upon reading it I noticed slightly feeling rejected because I knew what we were not, but I also noticed we were giving each other a tad bit more attention than what we believed each other deserved because of our arrangement.

In another conversation she told me that she liked me and my personality and that she wouldn't change anything about me but she wanted to enhance and add to my life. That conversation was also followed by a YouTube video link to Vedo's "Add to you." I instantly smiled, although I did not expect that. I feel like I connect very well with R&B music and have always said I wanted a love that feels like 90s R&B. Also, I'm always one to send song lyrics or even be in deep thought connecting a person, myself, and our dynamics in an R&B song, so for Skyy to send that to me felt again that she had somehow tapped into my soul.

3 HER lips and mine

We had been arguing this entire day between her telling me I'm too emotional, her being too emotional, my telling her she's too emotional, and us both still fighting our emotions. We had to work together later this evening. The levels of panic and anxiety I was experiencing felt to be at its ultimate highest to the point where I had tears in my eyes, both on my way to and while at work. I wear my emotions on my sleeve, so my mood was noticed by her and everyone around us. I had to hold it together, though, because we were both at work.

Apparently the tension enhanced a sexual feeling for something because not too much time had passed before I received a text from Skyy saying, "You're so beautiful right now."

Blood rushed through my veins reading her text because all I could think about was how I wanted to passionately release these endorphins my body was producing. I've always believed Skyy was beautiful, but her beauty was amplified under angry emotions. I'm not sure if it was the extra vulnerability I was most attracted to or the way she expressed herself and I could tap into how she was thinking and could see the world through her eyes when she explained her feelings. Whatever it was, I loved the thrill. It was something to always keep me on my feet, and coming from a life on the more conservative side, it was just exciting.

I responded, "No, you are beautiful." Then double texted, "May I have a kiss?" I knew a kiss would calm her and would soothe me. I also felt like I was in high school again sneaking away from class, but I just needed her in that moment. It's like my body was beginning to crave hers.

She answered my request by saying, "Come get it. I'm in the supply closet."

What did I do? I submitted to her orders, left my work area, asked my manager to cover until I came back and met Skyy in the supply closet. It took everything in me to keep this kiss a kiss for the sake of extremely limited privacy because we were at work. We couldn't do anything but gaze at each other and try to small talk as if we didn't know why the both of us were standing in this isolated space. Skyy dominantly snatched my arm and pulled me close to her, aligning our bodies as mirror images of each other because our heights are nearly perfect to each other. Her lips touched mine, and for a good ten seconds, my soul got lost again.

I got lost in how therapeutic this felt. I got lost in how much I did not want this encounter to ever end. I got lost in the fact that I was just feeling something more. My blood got warmer as it flowed euphorically through my veins. My eyes closed softly as if her touch was a drug that took me away. My fingers and toes got tingly. Hell, my heart probably skipped a beat.

When I regained my consciousness, I remember squeezing her ass and damn near soaking my panties. We stopped kissing. She looked me in the eyes in the most seductive manner and asked, "So are you going to stop acting crazy now?"

Submissively, I responded, "Yes I am."

She smiled at me, gave me a tap on my ass and said, "Ok, good. Now go back to work."

I walked out of the supply closet while she remained in that location to complete her task. I returned to my work station happy as ever; my body felt like I was a helium balloon floating into the open space. Every chance we got that night, we found some corner, some bathroom, some closet or empty isle to replay the scene. I guess we couldn't get past the enjoyment because our lips definitely made their way back to each other's about three times that night.

Conversations became a little deeper and I noticed I started to develop an addiction for her attention. I followed her nearly half the night helping her complete her work.

She told me, "You remind me of someone."

"Who?" I asked. "Thread lightly" I jokingly added.

She paused and sighed, then replied, "I've only been in love with one female, my ex of three years, and you remind me so much of her. You two are like twins."

We both smiled. I saw the interlocked female symbol with her ex's name on her neck. At this point, I'm soaking in every moment I can with her. I'm helping her clean the store for the night because I want her to get home and relax, but I also want her to stay here with me.

That night passed and we were still on board to hang out Friday night. Friday comes, and I'm thinking everything is too good to be true. Based on past experiences, totally unrelated to Skyy, I've learned not to get too excited or what could possibly change and not even happen, which in return would leave my feelings crushed and my confidence and self-esteem at its ultimate lowest. Most of all, I didn't want to face the person who would have been the reason I am feeling this way. It's a major issue I have between my pride and my vulnerability. Although immoral, out of character, and a huge flex, just in case this would be the case tonight, I wanted to beat her to it.

Looking back, a simple, "Good morning. I am looking forward to seeing you later today," text would have been just fine. Not just fine, it would have been the absolute genuine representation of my true feelings. Instead, I had to give an illusion that my attention was occupied by someone else.

I texted Skyy, "Hi. My ex popped up today. I'm helping her out with some things. I'll text you first. Don't text me." I went to work and we literally did not talk the whole day. Closer to 4:00pm, she texted me that she would start getting dressed.

I replied, "Ok. I'll be on my way once I get your address. She sent me her address and included "green," the safe code word we came up with that means pull up.

I texted her that I was on my way past the time that I was actually supposed to be at her house. She ended up calling me while I was on my way, but I did not want to talk about my being late and not respecting her time, so I did not answer until I arrived at her gate. She texted me that she was on her way.

Nervously but patiently, I waited for her to come out. Moments passed and there she was. I could see her through my rear view mirror, looking much like the meal I want to indulge in right now. To call her a snack would diminish the effect her presence had over me. She was way more than that quick gas station run for an instant hunger fix. Shorty was the last bite of steamed lobster tail you couldn't finish at the dinner table so you take it home along with the butter sauce.

She came out wearing a peachy colored, cheeky, one-piece romper with a thong underneath for a smooth seamless finish, her locs, up in a ponytail, a pretty colorful jelly purse and her black furry UGG sandals, with a jazz wood-tip black and mild cigar between her fingers. She smelled so sweet and had just the right amount of attitude with me. She tried not to look at me, and I tried not to look at her. I leaned over to give her a kiss as I grasped her face in my hand.

She leaned back, avoiding my kiss and said, "I don't know where your lips been."

I laughed because I knew my lips had not been anywhere but she didn't know at this moment that I was just fucking with her mind earlier this morning.

"No because I don't have my Carmex," she continued.

"We can stop and get you some Carmex. Where you want to stop?" I responded.

We stopped at Kroger, she told me that she liked Kroger and that was her favorite grocery store. I parked and she headed towards the store. "Do...you want me to go in with you, or wait in the car?" I awkwardly asked.

"Do you want to go in the store with me Starr? What kind of question is that?" She responded. I took that as a yes and went in the store with her. We shopped for Carmex and headed to the self-checkout. I remember wanting to pay for her Carmex, but not wanting to show her too much niceness too soon.

We made it by my house and I asked her the question every girl loves to hear, "You ate?" To me, and you, the reader may agree, this is the best foreplay to an amazing evening.

"I ate earlier." She responded. "What would you like to eat?" I added. In a soft under-her-breath tone she replied, "Pussy."

"What? You want what?" I smiled because I, too, wanted some pussy. I mean pussy was the reason while we were here in the first place.

I was surprised by the dominance she was exhibiting in that moment. I thought I heard her correctly but I wasn't sure. "What did you hear me say?" She questioned.

"Ummm, I don't know." I softly replied. I caught on to her and what she was doing. "You will get that later." I assured her. She smiled and we headed to one of the wing spots by my house.

We got out and went inside. "Don't you owe me a hug?" I asked Skyy. She came close to me and embraced me in her arms around my neck pushing her body close to mine. Feelings of happiness and pleasure rushed through my veins, the kind of feeling that also gets a girl's girl aroused. I caressed her waist and pulled her closer to me reciprocating the same embrace she had given me.

We each ordered a fried rice bowl. When it was time to pay, I realized that I left my card in my car. "Wait here, I'm going to get my card. You better not pay for it." I told her. She heard me and understood I wanted to be the one to pay for our food but also had the same desire. By the time I could make it back in, she had already paid for both of our food. "I thought I said not to pay for it?" I asked her in what I thought was a stern tone.

She smiled, then responded, "Oh, I thought you said to please pay for it." We both gazed at each other because I knew that's not what she heard, and she knew that's not what I said.

Usually, I have the dominant energy and like to be the one to take care of things like that, so I thought it was so sweet of her to reciprocate that energy. We got to the house which was nearly empty at the time. I had no living room furniture, but some bar stools, a bed, and the bathroom was fully decorated.

"Aww so you cleaned up and got it all nice for me? I like it?" she said while walking around to view the setup. I noticed there was one thing she was glued to more than anything, my vision board. While I was in the kitchen getting our dinner set up, she had gotten so quiet. I looked up and caught her thoroughly admiring my vision board. I smiled. I poured us some wine in my clear glass fish bowls, and we began to eat. I remember being so attracted and intrigued by her posture and etiquette while we ate. It was so correct, and it said so much about her. It was in this moment that I began to see her as this beautiful, sexy woman full of grace and poise. I felt that she had let me into her authentic soft side.

Conversations started to flow during dinner. "What if you catch feelings for me?" she asked.

"I'm not going to catch any feelings for you. Why do you keep thinking I'm going to catch feelings?" I responded.

"Because of the way I'm going to hold you and touch you." she said. I couldn't do anything in this moment but take a deep breath because she was probably right. In fact, whatever was happening in this exact moment was already bringing out some uncontrollable feelings. It was nothing that I was doing to make these feelings appear. It just....happened. Years from now I would learn that there will be several times where my feelings proved to be true, and I verbally acclaimed that they were non-existent. I spent a lot of time fighting and suppressing these feelings. I would wonder if the story would have turned out differently had I spoken up sooner or if I would have hidden the feelings longer or simply just let them go.

We finished dinner. We continued to pour and finish the bottle of wine. We talked, we flirted, we made out, left the house to buy some gas to smoke, took the long way back to the house, and, literally, for hours, got lost in the vibe. I enjoyed her company and felt so blessed to be a part of her angelic presence.

"I really want to fuck you, but I actually like you," she repeatedly said a few times that night.

I remember asking her why we couldn't be together if we vibe so well together. Our connection felt so magnetic. It felt intimate, romantic and platonic at the same time. She felt like the best friend I've always known, the sister I grew up with, the soul mate I've manifested, and the love I needed. In one day this girl became the air I needed to survive. Figuratively speaking, but somewhat literally because her absence over time continued to bring about a lonesome feeling within myself. She told me that in her head I was hers, so basically, I couldn't have anyone else on the same level as her, not a girl anyways. I agreed and didn't ever feel like this pact we made would ever be a problem because, in fact, she was all that I wanted.

To confirm that I was enjoying myself immensely, I could not remember the last time I touched my phone or knew where it was. When I did get a hold of the time, it was 2am. I knew our chemistry mixed so well together, but when we walked to the gas station and people saw our chemistry, we drew so much attention, attention that I had never received before. You would think we were public figures, and people had recognized us in a public place. People kept looking at us as we shared displays of affection.

Then people started adding commentary like, "Are you two sisters?" "Damn y'all are fine." "Can I join?"

I told Skyy that we would need security with us if we were going to continue to hang out in public like that. People were so invested. I know they felt a chemistry that was strong between us, but I didn't know how they would conduct themselves around us. I made an attempt to hide my anxiousness. We got what we needed from the store and started our walk back home. Even on our way home, men stopped their cars, blew their horns, and tried to talk out the window to us. Between the influence I was under, her, our being outside, I was so overstimulated, and I honestly could not remember the route back home. Skyy remained calm as she laughed that I genuinely could not remember the way back. I stopped in the middle of the walk and just started hugging her and kissing on her neck.

Skyy whispered to me, "Why are you starting with me? Don't start anything you cannot finish. She remembered, and we made it back home. We never touched the cards I had brought us to play. We didn't need anything to fill the time as I anticipated we would.

4 Purely passion

When Skyy and I got back in the house, I couldn't resist. I started to kiss her and caress her. I pushed her to the wall, grabbed her hands and pinned them both to the wall, interlocking my fingers between hers. She switched positions with me and pinned me to the wall with a quite stronger grip than what I had on her. She looked me in my eyes and said this is how I like to be handled. Showing me that I basically needed to apply a little more pressure because she didn't like that soft shit. We made our way to my bedroom.

Our eyes met again. "Starr, is this what you want to do?" She asked me.

I was so nervous, but I was so sure this is what I wanted. I took a deep breath and said, "Yes, I want you."

She straddled me and put her hair in a high ponytail. I got her out of that one-piece romper and started sucking her nipples. I continued to kiss her softly until my face made its way perfectly between the warmth of her thighs.

For me, this was my very first encounter with a woman. She made me feel as if I had done everything right. I didn't get the vibe that I was "doing the damn thing," but I also didn't get the vibe that it was not enjoyable. She was willing to teach and I was willing to explore and learn her. Her hands guided my head while her fingers made soft strokes through my braids. My hands touched her inner thighs and slowly rubbed her lower stomach, adding a gentle pressure. My eyes attempted to gaze into hers but couldn't do anything but roll back in pure enjoyment. I lifted my head from this sweet flowing feminine aroma of endless waters and positioned my body to scissor or tribe with her. Hers against mine and mine against hers. This one felt unmatched. I was in the dominant position, so here I could look into her face as I simultaneously grinded on her. We both moaned in enjoyment and pleasure.

Then...her phone rang. It was him, her boyfriend. The first time she didn't answer, but I told her to answer the second time. She answered in a chill and innocent tone and proceeded to say that she was okay and was having a great time. To add to the thrill, I resumed grinding against her to see if she could maintain her poise, but she hit me signaling that she did not like that, so I stopped.

When she ended the phone call, we continued and she reciprocated. I melted the moment her lips touched my pussy. From her tongue, she whispered me a love poem in French. I've experienced this act from the opposite gender, but this encounter had no comparison to what I had felt in the past. I felt the intimate embrace of her soul everywhere. My toes curled, my eyelashes tickled, and my pussy responded with a flood of ocean waves. Her touch amplified the euphoria. She was my natural ecstasy pill in human form. We concluded our session and she asked for a hot towel. I'm thinking, "Just a hot towel? You can have my social security number if you want." I was locked in. I was hooked. Skyy was my bad habit I didn't want to break.

As an act of adoration, I put her panties back on for her. "Oh wow. This is the treatment I get now?" she asked, smiling and allowing me to spoil her with this queen treatment.

"Most definitely," I responded.

"Do you have any regrets?" she asked again.

"I have none." I told her. "I'm glad we chose to move forward with it." I added.

She agreed. While she rolled another joint, I found my phone and started ordering her an edible arrangement to be delivered to work the next day for her. I kept trying to hide my screen while trying not to hold my phone too long so she wouldn't think I was texting anyone in her presence. I felt like she had seen enough of my asshole side, and I felt emotionally safe to start showing her a little more honest vulnerability. I was happy but I did feel sadness coming on due to it being time for Skyy to return home. I knew that along with our plans for the next day she also had the delivery of the edible arrangements to look forward to, so I anticipated her reaction when she got them.

The ride to her house was sweet. We reflected on the day, listened to music, and when we got to her house, shared a kiss and said good night. Skyy was a little anxious at how she would enter the house. She contemplated hanging out outside before she walked in the house and just proceeding to walk in the house. She later told me that she ended up smoking outside for a while before entering her home. I later learned that she cried and told her boyfriend that we had sex and that she apologized, and he forgave her.

The next day, I didn't have to work. I dedicated my entire day to prep for our plans that upcoming evening. My hair was already done-braided in long blonde tribal braids. I booked a lash appointment, nails to match the lemon juice color design that I suggested Skyy get earlier that week, and make up that day. I also had my outfit scheduled to be picked up from the tailor too. I wore a purple Raptors jersey with the Top 3 5s, and some red Jordan socks. To me, wardrobe is where I thrive, so I was more ready to show my style outside of work.

She texted me stating that she had an amazing time the previous night and asked me will I do it again. I told her yes, as long as she was willing I would. I got another text with her being surprised that she got the edible arrangement and her saying thank you. She was so happy and it was so unexpected for her. She learned that gestures like this one continued to happen over the course of us knowing each other. I've always loved how she shows gratitude when I do nice things for her and how sometimes it shifted her mood when she was down, so it motivated me to continue.

I made sure this night I was ready before she even got off of work. Skyy would not have to wait for me this time because I was too eager to see her. I went to pick her up again.

"Girl, he knows we had sex," she said.

"How does he know?" I asked."

Her response was, "You don't even want to know." I didn't ask for details beyond this point because it honestly wasn't any of my business. "I got a surprise for us tonight," she said, "something to get us on cloud 9 and enjoy the vibe tonight." It was a blunt her boyfriend rolled up for us because he wanted us to have a good time.

We arrived at the first hookah bar and waited in line. She played in my hair, held me from behind, hugged me from the front, and just kept showing me so much affection while we waited in line. We ended up not staying due to the long wait, so we headed to another spot. We smoked the blunt before we went in, and once we entered, the attention started again. This time, I'm away from home in an unfamiliar environment and in protective mode. We ordered drinks, found a spot on the wall, danced, and vibe to the music. When the night was over, we headed home and agreed that we both enjoyed the night.

The next day we continued to talk and text. I believe we had a few minutes in our work schedule to overlap which allowed us to see each other for a little while. Seeing her at work after getting to know her personally now would hit differently than seeing her at work previously. She told me during our weekend together that it would be hard for her not to call me "baby" at work since that's the name that flowed so naturally once we got closer. It would also be hard for us to communicate that much at work overall due to the time, mandatory face masks, the flow of business was always at its peak, and trying to hide the whole thing from everyone to keep our matters private.

The following Monday I went to work at my first job at the hospital, and she was home until the evening. I received a video from her. Seeing her name come across my phone always made me happy; seeing it was a video made me even happier. I stepped away from my desk to view it. Skyy had recorded the sweetest most vulnerable confessional video. She was in her home lying on her bed.

The video stated, "I know you're at work right now, but I'm thinking about you, and honestly, I really, really like you. Like, I like you a lot! I didn't expect myself to like you as much as I like you with the situation I have going on. I didn't think I could just like someone so much, and I know it's soon but, it is what it is. And it's more difficult for me because I kind of don't want to turn my back on someone who has been with me through everything when I felt like I needed somebody, and I couldn't do it by myself. I just wish I could have my cake and my pie and eat it too, about you and him being a certain way. I think you're smart. I think you're beautiful. I think you're so attractive. I love your smile, and I'm so big on smiles. I love your skin tone color, how you dress, how you even talk. I love your personality. I think we connect and that's so good on so many levels."

Mid-way into the video, I immediately started crying uncontrollably. This was so genuine, and I felt every word. Well, I felt some of her words. I remember viewing the video and feeling a combination of emotions. One, I was happy that she was expressing her true feelings to me and that the feelings were mutual, but I also didn't understand how she felt torn between us both. In my head, I had already given her reasons why she could just uproot her life. My overthinking also made me believe she wasn't happy in her relationship. My lack of understanding of her perspective made it difficult for me to respect her view as well. I thought Skyy was wanting things her way, and even after I said no, she was trying to convince me to change my mind. My emotions even took me out of belief for a moment, and I started to question if she really felt these words. I texted her back telling her that the video was the sweetest gesture, and I'm glad our feelings were in the same place. She then invited me over to smoke later that day and meet her boyfriend. I declined, disrespectfully.

"No. You just don't get it do you?" I texted back.

"Get what? I'm just inviting you over to smoke. He is not trying to do anything that you already said no to, but you don't have to if you don't want to."

I continued to decline the invites for a while. They were worded in different ways, one of which he asked to go to Six Flags with us for Labor Day. His presence would interfere with Skyy's and my energy and we wouldn't have a great time, or she would act a certain way around him, and I would feel rejected, or the focus would be so sexual, and I would be uncomfortable around him was my reasoning for the invitation declines to all hang out as one. The trip to Six Flags started out fun. I picked Skyy up from her house and we headed to Target to purchase some last minute items. She brought me some sunglasses and earrings. We put our bags in a locker, rode rides together, and ate around the park. Apparently we didn't retrieve our bags from the locker in enough time before the park closed so my keys got locked in the park overnight. Skyy was talking to Solar to pick us up, I was about to book an Uber, but didn't want us to split up with a stranger. After she confirmed with Solar to pick us up, I called my cousin to pick me up, without telling Skyy. When Solar arrived, I told Skyy that I had a different ride. My cousin arrived shortly after him. Skyy was upset with me but we hugged, kissed and each of us went home.

Between Solar feeling excluded and me wanting to see Skyy every chance she had some free time, it did cause some friction. She told me that I couldn't take all of her off days and that she had to spend time with him too. She also said his feelings and my feelings towards the whole thing were upsetting her and putting her in the middle and that she couldn't handle trying to keep us both happy.

5 Unconditional...love?

We decided to call everything off. I deleted all text messages and pictures as this felt like she and I both meant what we were saying and that we were sure we would not have to revisit this matter ever again. Before we made it official though Skyy wanted to vibe one more time. We went out for drinks at Cirque. I apologized to her for calling her out of her name during an argument. She shared with me that she was feeling guilty with how our relationship flourished while she was still in a relationship with Solar. She told me I deserved better and that we could still be friends. I respected her thought. I was having fun with what we were doing but she was right. I asked her to make a promise with me. "Promise me you won't get engaged, married or pregnant without considering me first." I told her. She promised me as neither of those thoughts were on her mind. She asked for one last kiss and with tears in my eyes, I kissed her. I tried to make this kiss last because after this meant no more. For months I survived off of Skyy's kisses so I didn't know how I was going to manage. When I drove her home we stayed in the car some more and started making out.

On another day Skyy was upset, crying and text me. Without thinking my first reaction was that I needed to physically see her. I went to her house and told her to come outside to talk to me. She didn't though. She told me we would talk later. My feelings for her grew stronger. I wondered if it was too early for me to love her, or if she loved me back. I couldn't be the first to say it. "What if she was waiting on me?" I thought. I thought of a way to ask her about her feelings but when we got together things flowed differently in a good way. If we felt it there was not a need to discuss it. I rested on the fact that it will happen at the right time.

We sat in the park one night and was having a discussion and out of nowhere, just started kissing. "What was the kiss about?" She asked me. "It was just a kiss." I told her. "No, I felt some extra feelings in that kiss versus the other kisses. Tell me something Starr." She said. This was the time to tell her that I loved her. She already knew though. When my words got lost, she helped pull them out of me. "Do you love me?" she asked. We agreed to vulnerability but I was still fighting my feelings. "Should I love you?" I asked her back. "Am I worth loving?" she asked me. I told her yes, she was worth it, because she was! "I do love you Skyy." I told her and she told me that she loved me too.

It wasn't until later when we shared a conversation that helped me connect the dots from her past and understand who she was now that I realized that when I first felt love for her it was still romantic love. After learning more about her I realized that more than anything Skyy needed loyalty and someone who she could trust, because she never had that. She needed a real friend! It was easy for me to love someone I liked and wanted to be with but loving her knowing that she would never choose me was unconditional. It would mean I loved her when she did the total opposite of what I wanted her to do. Loving is easy, but loving unconditionally is a task. The moment that I accepted that we may not work out romantically and I was fine with that made me realized that my love was true because all conditions were lifted.

6 Considering poly

One thing I did notice and admired about Skyy was her persistence in going for what she wanted. She had confidence that she would get everything she asked for, and she wasn't wrong about it. She knew Solar would not tell her no and that I was almost at a point where I wouldn't either. If her hard approach didn't work, her soft approach would be sure to. No matter how many invites I declined to hang out with both her and Solar, she never stopped asking.

As our relationship progressed, I thought that I could be more open to chilling with them both at least once. He was clearly an important part of her life, and she had shown me that I was, too. Without telling her, I made the decision that the next time they invited me out I would say yes.

I met him once prior at their house unexpectedly. I came over to see Skyy one evening and she invited me in to smoke. He wasn't there at first, but he ended up coming home while I was there. They seemed to be at odds on this particular day, so it was a sort of dry meeting. Not too long after, on another day while I was at work and Skyy was home, she sent me a text to hang out with her and Solar one night for drinks. I couldn't help but to think about how she and I fucked in the park by their house about a week prior. My conscience was bad because she had to wear makeup on her neck and she mentioned me doing it on purpose, but I really didn't.

To her surprise I didn't rebuttal to the invite, and I even picked the place for us to go. We ended up going back to Cirque. I didn't feel nervous about this night at all; in fact, I was looking forward to a great time. I viewed this night as a way to bring Skyy and me closer by listening to her and considering her wants. At one point, I started to feel bad that I always used to put her in the position where she had to choose between Solar and me. It was really hard for her and made her cry before because she honestly could not choose. The more I got to know her, the more I evolved and became open-minded. I started to be more understanding to things that once sounded or felt weird to me in regards to this whole situation.

When we arrived at the lounge, I was so happy to see Skyy. Like she always has, she greeted me with the biggest, most intimate hug while Solar and I exchanged what's ups. They wore outfits to coordinate with their matching black Timberlands and I wore an outfit to go with my khaki Timberlands. While we waited on our reservations we went to Solar's truck to smoke. Skyy sat between us and I couldn't help but notice a different type of happiness I had never seen before on her. Her smile appeared a little brighter this night, her embrace lasted a little longer, and her laugh a little louder. She had this dreamy Disneyland sparkle in her eyes that I kept gazing into.

Everything I never understood about why this moment was so important for her became clear. Solar felt inclusive and treated us both so well. Everything he did for Skyy, he did for me. I wondered if they had a conversation about their plans for this night. If they did, they did a great job of setting it up. I felt comfortable enough to let my hair down and enjoy the vibe. Skyy took pictures and recorded videos of all of us together that night while we lived in the moment. She kept saying "I'm so happy" throughout the night.

Skyy and I shared some fried shrimp and fries, and then we raced to see who could finish our cocktails first before we left. As I was about to pay for my food, Solar stopped me and took care of everything. One of the conversations we laughed and talked about at the table was how Skyy creates her own UNO rules.

They invited me over to their house afterwards. We agreed that Skyy would ride with me so I wouldn't drive alone after we had been drinking. On our way to the car, Skyy pretended that she was going to do a trust fall. She asked, "If I fall back which, one of you will catch me?"

We all looked at each other and I said, "Both of us will." That was my way of telling Skyy she had us both and that I kind of liked it.

I remember thinking that this is a vibe I could probably get used to. Solar was way cooler than I imagined him to be. He had a sense of confidence that he was comfortable in his role to her; therefore, my presence didn't bother him. In fact, he seemed to like having me around. I like to believe that my presence brought out a better side of her. I enjoyed being around them both. We smoked some more, turned on some music, and Skyy and I had some more wine. She brought out the UNO cards and we played about 3 rounds. Years later, UNO cards at the house, weed and alcohol would be a normal vibe for us. This vibe was even better at their house than at the lounge.

After the last round of UNO, Skyy and I teamed up, trying not to make each other lose. We stopped playing; she definitely did make her own rules to that game. I remember Solar left the living room to go use the restroom, and Skyy started dancing across the room. I love everything about dancers and had recently found out that she enjoyed dancing. I had been asking her to show me her skills for a while prior to this day.

When I thought the night couldn't get any better, she started dancing on my lap to "Inside" by Jacquees. I thought she would jump off my lap when Solar came back into the living room, but she didn't. I just knew he was going to be upset about what he was seeing but he wasn't. Instead he was hyping us both up. I felt like I was getting a VIP dance at the strip club. The song ended and it was my turn to dance for her. I'm no dancer but under the influence I get really freaky. I prefer slow music to grind to so I told her to replay the same song. I danced on her while she gripped my waist and rubbed my ass. Solar watched as he enjoyed the vibe then said, "Damn I want my turn to."

I told Skyy to go dance with him first; then she cued me to dance with him after. "She thick in those jeans, isn't she, bae?" Skyy asked Solar.

"Hell yea." He responded to her rubbing on my ass too. The song ended again but we were having fun so I was trying to keep the fun going.

"Now it's your turn to dance to a faster song," I told Skyy as I grabbed the remote and started playing Trina's "Look Back at Me".

"OK, I have to go put on my joggers. They are more comfortable to dance in. I'll be back," she said and left to go to her and Solar's bedroom.

The intro of the song was already playing during her wardrobe change, but by the time the beat dropped, she was running back in the living room as if it was her stage. This girl did not put on any joggers. She came around the corner in the sexiest pair of black G-string thongs and a shirt.

My mouth dropped. I was excited but shocked at the same time. Skyy danced the entire song, and let me tell you, home girl can dance. From this day forward, I have always given her well-deserved flowers in that area. She danced so professionally, and she worked the room with Solar and me; dividing her attention so equally, both of us felt like her main. She made her ass clap, she threw it in a circle, and gave it her all. "Is this the same ass that be hiding in those jeans?" I thought to myself.

I looked over at Solar and he was just enjoying the performance and rolling another joint. This moment awakened a grown and sexy side of my womanhood. I stared in awe of her physique. I admired how she carried herself as a woman and was thoroughly even more attracted to her entire aura. She had it all ... the crazy, the sexy, and the cool. We were bonding again on another level that we haven't reached before. I was convinced that she was magical. Even though we spent a lot of time together, she had given me a lot of my firsts. No two moments felt the same and that was where the thrill came in.

After her performance, she went to put on some pink biker shorts and laid on the couch. While we were all lying on the couch, she texted me.

For her contact in my phone I had a special ringtone for her text alerts and phone calls so when I heard my phone sound I was thinking about what she was trying to say. She nudged me and said, "Check your phone." The text read. "Eat my pussy."

I immediately started sweating in panic. I rubbed my forehead and squinted my eyes to make sure this was really what I was reading. I was drunk and the moment felt right, but this could all turn out bad if everyone is not as free as me right now. I couldn't play like I didn't read the text; she was looking right at me waiting on me to make a move. She texted again. "I want you."

By this point, I was starting to get a little distracted because what's going on with me is about to be a boomer for everyone. Mother Nature came to make her visit earlier that morning. I knew once I backed out that Skyy would think this is something I'm not interested in. I was interested, I just needed a rain check on this night. I needed to whisper in her ear and give her that one disclaimer so that she can understand. At the same time, I need my actions to show that I was down.

I started rubbing on her then I took her shorts off and submitted. It was more fun than it was weird. I intentionally tried not to come up for air simply for the fact that I did not want to look at Solar's face right now. "What if he's mad about this? What if she doesn't enjoy it from me but enjoys it from him? What if I can't handle seeing them fuck each other?" I thought to myself.

"Damn, Starr, save some for me." I heard Solar say. This would be the second time he mentioned it was his turn or reminded us not to forget about him. I stopped and let him take over then went to kiss Skyy but she was trying to get me to show Solar some attention.

"Go to our bedroom." She told me. I went in there and she came behind me.

"My cycle is on," I whispered to her in disappointment, but she didn't slow down. She was still demanding me. Solar came in and attempted to join again. "I'm trying not to mess up the bed, at least go get a towel." I said. I wanted this experience to flow naturally and it seemed to not be flowing at all. Skyy started to tell Solar to get out. When I heard her tell him to get out, I was scared to proceed to do anything to her because I knew he would be upset and feel left out.

He exited the room and said' "OK. Y'all have your fun."

I sobered up and called it off. Skyy thought I was lying about my reason, and to ease her mind I had to show her I wasn't just saying that for no reason. I ended up crashing on their couch that night because it was too late and I was too intoxicated to drive myself home. I worried if they were mad at me or mad at each other. I was sure I could make it up to them the following week if I needed to redeem myself. The ménage à trois amongst us was a new fantasy of mine.

The next morning, I woke up to go home, and Skyy let me out. When I got home, she apologized that she was sorry for the night, but I told her I didn't have a problem with anything that night other than the fact that I couldn't move forward. What I thought were opportunities to open that door again in the future just turned out to be empty signs that were far from the chance ever presenting itself again.

7 SCORNED

We returned to work the following week. The more we bonded outside of work, the harder it became to work together. Even though we counted it as a chance to see each other, sometimes it wasn't good. A new girl had started at work this week and Skyy had to train her on a night she was scheduled to stay and deep clean until 3am. Skyy asked me to stay and deep clean with her, so I did. I was going to stay anyways because I was jealous of anyone who appeared to be taking any kind of attention from Skyy. The new coworker had invited her out after work, so Skyy invited me too. Did I really want to hang out with the new girl at work and her husband? Absolutely not. Did Skyy? She did and she wanted me to be present, so I agreed to go. After work we followed the new coworker to her house which was close by the job, just like Skyy's house. On the way to a new coworker's house, Skyy and I shared our reservations about the night. We were both just a little socially anxious hanging out with new people, but we knew that we had each other present. She wouldn't leave me, I wouldn't leave her, and if we had to enjoy each other's vibe amid everyone else that's what we would do.

We walked into their house, and I knew that Skyy's and my vibe, as I have known it to be, was incompatible with theirs. We were drinkers and smokers. The new coworker and her husband were pill poppers. They started explaining to us what pills they had and how each made them feel and gave us each one. We both were on the same page in not wanting to take it, so we just put them in our pockets. We ended up having to go to the car for something, leaving the couple inside so we had some private time to talk again. We talked about how we are not going to take the pill and how their vibe was different, but we would make the best of the night. We said we would ride in my car together just in case we want to leave earlier since I did have to go to my first job in about 5 hours. When we got back in the house, our new coworker gave Skyy an outfit to wear, I wore what I had on at my 1st job, and we headed out. I noticed the couple were the pushy and convincing type. They said that parking at the lounge where we were going was going to be a hassle and that we should ride with them. We got in the car and were literally holding hands in the back seat all the way until we found a seat at the lounge. When we got to the lounge, the crowd, to me, felt equally weird. They were neither drunk nor high. The vibe was identical to the vibe at the house. I wasn't feeling this. I could not chill somewhere I wasn't comfortable. We ordered a round of drinks and I remember hitting the blunt a few times it came around. I probably should have passed on the last two rotations, but I didn't. By now, I was starting to get cross faded.

Mid drink, the husband of our new coworker came around asking if we wanted another round of drinks. I asked for water. He responded, "Water? No let's get her another crown and cranberry." The drinks arrived but I never saw them being made so I didn't drink mine and kept watching to make sure Skyy didn't drink hers. Everyone seemed to have aggressive demeanors in that place. My focus was to protect Skyy. She and coworker were having a conversation, and I could slightly hear them. The coworker was telling her how she hustles, and I heard her say something else about the pills. I started to get angry because they were being too pushy on the pills and drinks. When a guy tried to talk to Skyy, she told him she was with me, and he didn't believe her, so she kissed me. The husband saw her kiss me and started flirting with us both asking us what we were doing after. I was sure Skyy knew I was ready to go. The look we talked about giving each other when one was ready to go home, I was giving her. The crow grew and I started to get extremely paranoid. I know I was under the influence, but I also understood my inner me was rejecting this environment.

I looked up Uber or Lyft on my phone and told Skyy I was ready to go. I asked Skyy to call Solar to pick us up. When he got on the phone you could hear the panic in my voice. I was begging Solar to please come pick us up. She said she had to use the restroom and I started grabbing her things. I heard a male voice ask to go to the bathroom with us. Others were trying to get me to leave our things behind, I guess to indicate that we were coming back, or I may have thought we were about to get robbed. When we got outside, Skyy started crying and said she didn't like that I panicked. She was embarrassed that we left so abruptly and said that the only reason I reacted the way I did was because I was too high. She told me that she protects me, I don't need to protect her. I told her no; I protect you because that's what I do well. Solar pulled up and took us to him and Skyy's house. When I saw his truck pull up, I felt an instant relief. We started telling him about the night and when we got in their house, I took a shower. Skyy gave me a toothbrush, some clean clothes and talked to me while I took a shower. I took a nap and she and Solar took me to get my car a few hours later. The only thing I had time to do was drive to my house, do a wardrobe change and head back to work.

The aftereffects of the night were all over me, I couldn't function at work, so I left early. New coworker put Skyy and I in a group chat that morning asking us if we were ok and apologized for the night being so crazy and even suggested a calmer place another time. Skyy and I discussed that we wouldn't hang with them anymore. They were cool people, just not the cool we were into. I never responded to the group chat, and I assumed Skyy didn't either. When I left work early, I went back to Skyy's house because I just wanted to be under her. She would be the one to make me feel better, her company alone. We spent time talking as usual and I went to my house to celebrate an early Christmas with my group of friends at the time. My friends left and I noticed that Skyy and I didn't have our usual talk before bedtime or exchange good nights. I assumed she fell asleep because she mentioned not feeling well and being sleepy earlier that day as well.

Another day passed and we were back to our normal conversations. I saw where Skyy posted a story update on Instagram, but since we were always with each other, or sleep or at work, I never thought to open the story. I worked at Publix that evening and she did not. I finally watched her story a little before the 24-hour mark where it expires. He posted her, Solar, the new coworker, and coworker's husband back at the same place enjoying themselves. So, the night before when I was at home waiting to hear her voice before I went to sleep, she was out with the same people we said we wouldn't be with. Not only that, but she was with me previously the same day and never mentioned anything that happened after the group text was sent out.

The over thinker in me automatically assumed they took the pills and were all swinging and that Skyy had replaced me with the new coworker. My temper knew no medium, from zero I went all the way to one hundred. I called Skyy yelling and cussing at her about how she never mentioned anything to me but was back hanging out with this girl the whole time. Anytime I expressed myself to this level Skyy reminded me that I am not her girlfriend and that she can do whatever she wants, but when I acted like I was single and did whatever I wanted it was an issue to her. No, we weren't established girlfriends, but the understanding we had didn't permit what Skyy was doing, and she knew that.

For me the phone conversation wasn't enough, I told Skyy that I was on my way to her home. My shift at work wasn't over but I clocked out and told my manager I had to leave and rushed out of the store. Skyy told me not to come to her house because she wasn't home. I went anyways and told her I would wait for her. She told me that if I was there when she got there, we would fight. I arrived and put in the gate code and she and Solar pulled up after me. Skyy jumped out of the car to approach me and Solar jumped out, grabbed her and directed her back in the car. Skyy was so upset but I didn't care because so was I. I didn't care if we fought, I wanted to. My anger caused me to black out. I couldn't believe Skyy did this to me. The person I thought I grew to know was showing me that it's a lot that I didn't know. The understanding I thought we had she seemed to have taken advantage of it. I was crushed. This was the ultimate betrayal. From this moment my love for her would no longer be pure but guarded.

The trust was broken. I stayed on Skyy's doorstep for about thirty minutes this night. She kept asking me to leave, but I didn't. I felt like I was owed an apology or explanation, but she wasn't willing to give. This tension amongst us gave me an arousal, so I wanted to sex it out too. Madness enhanced Skyy's beauty and increased my desire for her. The police threats couldn't get me to leave either. The only one who was successful in getting me to leave and go home was Solar getting the phone from Skyy and telling me to go home.

I cried all the way to my house. I couldn't help but to think back on all the intimate moments we had and all the talks and promises we made to each other. How could Skyy feel so indifferent about keeping this away from me and about not having me around anymore? I tried to call her, but she blocked me. I needed to vent. I wanted to talk with someone who wouldn't judge me and someone who would understand me. I called my grandma. I told her everything- how much I loved Skyy, how I felt betrayed by her and how I snapped.

Her response calmed me.

"No one can tell you how to feel. I tell people all the time, when you have been dragged through the mud, I will be there at the end to clean you up. If you choose to go back and get dragged again, I will be on the other end to clean you up. I've never loved a woman, but I've heard that a woman can love you the way you have never been loved, and can hurt you the way you have never been hurt." She told me.

Not having communication with Skyy nor spending time with her opened the door for depression to make its entrance. For weeks I woke up anxious and went to sleep in tears. During the day I couldn't focus at work, I barely wanted to interact with people, I stopped eating. The only thing I could find to bring me some relief from feeling so down was smoking and drinking. Weed, black and mild, and alcohol were the fueling source for my body for about two weeks. I lost weight visibly and I cut back on interacting with the world. I had no interest nor energy to do anything but barely made it to work, perform at a minimum effort and go home to indulge in more "comfort cravings" and go to sleep.

To make matters worse, Christmas and New Year's came and left, and we still didn't resolve anything. The Jubilee 11s was the holiday drop that year and I copped us both a pair for our first Christmas since we liked to dress like twins. I still emailed her e-gift cards to Starbucks, Bath and Body Works and Target to still get her something for Christmas and express my sincerities. I couldn't even share that moment with her. Time helped initiate the healing process for me. Thankfully, I regained my appetite because smoking and drinking had me always feeling sick. I got more quality sleep and was able to put my better face on for work and to reconnect with some friends. On New Year's Day I purchased a new car and things started to align in my favor. I got a bonus at work and a pay increase, a customer even tipped me 100.00 one night at the store, I met new friends who I would spend time with and my whole perspective on life was optimistic.

Our work schedules overlapped a few times during the time when we were not speaking to each other. I noticed her and the new coworker made extra efforts to annoy me or make me feel jealous when we all worked together. It bothered me until it didn't. I stopped caring and I didn't get in between their plans. If one delayed their break to coordinate with the other, I let them. Skyy cut her hair and came in the store one day. If she wanted a priceless reaction of what I thought of her new look, I gave her that. I couldn't hide my thoughts, she walked by, and you would think I saw a goddess. Skyy looked stunning in her locs, but the low fade aesthetic was beyond attractive. She looked like a royal goddess. The cut highlighted her high cheek bones, and she had the perfect facial bone structure for the haircut. I absolutely loved it! I smiled at her, and I saw her smile back.

The only reason I didn't speak to her was because when the drama started between us, she asked me to leave her alone. I thought if I had missed my opportunity to break the ice. I didn't have to think too long. One of our friends at the job came up to me and said "Skyy texted me and she told me to tell you it's not nice to stare." I laughed that she even acknowledged that. "Tell Skyy I love her too." I told him. Her texted her and I was the happiest woman again. It wasn't much but it was a start, she paid attention to me, even if for a little while, it was enough for me to relish in. We worked together again soon after, for multiple hours.

Skyy does this thing where she talks in a volume loud enough for me to hear her when I'm not in the conversation she's having. She was purchasing a 4 pack Starbucks Mocha flavored Frappuccino drink but only wanted 1. The previous day I purchased a four pack because she started me liking those drinks too. I kept mine in the employee fridge in the breakroom. "Is there a way I can just buy one? I don't want to buy the whole 4 pack." She asked the cashier. I was close by working on something else. "I will sale you one of mine. It's already chilled." I inserted in the conversation. She smiled and put the four pack down and asked me how much. We made eye contact and smiled at each other. The kind of smile that said, I miss you. I told her 2.00 and she gave it to me. I told her where they were, she went upstairs and came back down. Still working on two different tasks but in close proximity of one another, she stopped her work and came to me and asked, "Why?" I looked confused because I didn't really know what she was talking about. "What do you mean?" I asked her. "Let's go talk outside." I added. "Why did you have to go crazy and mess up everything we had, all because you thought someone was stepping on your toes when no one ever came close to stepping on your toes?" she responded. "So, are you seeing her? Do you like her?" I asked her back without answering her question. "Fuck no!" she answered.

I couldn't handle this conversation, not here and not now. I have a thing, something like a fetish with intense conversations and Skyy's mad face. They make me very weak and automatically get me hot sexually. I seemed to have forgotten everything I wanted to say. I walked away from her and she pulled me back to her. Those two actions alone reassured me that we would rekindle. Skyy came across so passionately about not liking that we were not seeing each other anymore. "So where from here?" I asked her. She said she didn't know and left to go on her break. The timing was perfect for us to resolve our issues because her 25th birthday was approaching, and we planned to celebrate her birthday really big. I already had her birthday gifts purchased; I just didn't know how I was going to get them to her if we weren't talking. We talked a little throughout the week and I got her a mini surprise everyday leading up to her actual birthday. She told me that she wanted to invite me to her birthday party, but she didn't know how Solar would feel. I told her we could celebrate separately but she said it was her day and since she really wanted me to be present, then that's what was going to happen.

She didn't have a cake purchased so I reached out to a well know baker and got her some Tequila infused cupcakes made. I got my hair done and picked up the cake one night after work to deliver to Skyy's house the night before the party along with the box that I wrapped all her presents in. She met me outside when I arrived at her house after midnight, and we shared the first moments of her birthday together in my car. We danced, listened to music, took pictures and videos and she opened the box filled with all her favorites. Fighting to hold back happy tears, she appreciated how I stepped for her birthday, and I enjoyed seeing her so happy.

She told me I had to apologize to Solar for making a scene at their house. I agreed that an apology was an appropriate gesture so I went inside and gave Solar a sincere apology and asked if we could come together to help make Skyy's birthday special for her. He accepted and we moved forward with the party the following day. I wasn't done showing out for Skyy though. I felt like I was making up for some lost time, so I stopped to by the liquor store to buy bottles- Stella Rosa wine for me, Belaire Champagne for Skyy, and Hennessey per Solar's request because everywhere else was sold out, then headed to Skyy's house. I was told that the new coworker, her husband and other coworkers would be present. I was fine with that, but a little apprehensive to see everyone.

My plans were to get lit but not too lit. I wanted to get lit enough to have fun but not get too drunk. I hate that feeling. That was my reason for the wine. I was going to pour it in a red cup and just chill the whole night, engage in conversation, play whatever games and be present in the moment. I would not be to stand offish and act sober. Soon as I walked into the house, I took a shot. I do not remember if it was brown or white, but I mixed that night. Skyy's male best friend was my biggest influencer. I was able to pour my cup of wine before the party got too crowded. Her best friend called shot o' clock again with the Hennessey. I saw a Hennessey and Stella Rosa Black cocktail on Instagram before so instead of taking my second shot I mixed it with my wine and sipped on it.

I was in about two blunt rotations throughout the party too. Skyy found me and asked me to tell Solar to make her another drink-something he mixed up. I ended up asking him to make me one too. Usually when it is just Skyy and I out, she helped me monitor my alcohol intake and would make me stop drinking when she felt I had enough. That night she had guests to entertain, she was lit herself, and we were already in the house so that did not happen. The alcohol was helping my nerves from being around all these people, but the weed got me too faded. I was beyond drunk. I remember smiling at Skyy and admiring how happy and beautiful she looked during the party, and I remember giving someone my debit card to buy pizza but by the time the pizza arrived, Skyy and the other girls were holding my hair back over the toilet. I was so embarrassed. I really wanted to go home but I was too sick to do anything, including leave out the bathroom. I told the girls to leave me there, but they kept coming in to check on me. None of my friends even knew I had started back talking to Skyy, so I did not want to call anyone to come pick me up that late plus Skyy did not want anyone to know where her house was. I had to crash at their house again. I felt bad like ruined Skyy's night because she was really by my side asking sure I was ok as much as she could.

I visited my dad's house for the weekend, and I wanted to spend more time with Skyy when I got back home. She did not want to go out anywhere, so I went over to her house with her and Solar. The love and energy were so strong between us we also had fun, even when we were not doing anything. When I missed her, just a little of her company always made me happy and gave me what I needed to get through the days. Solar cooked for us and Skyy taught me how to play checkers. She told me that Solar taught her. I did not stay too long before it was time to hug, say good night and head to my house. We were doing good, but I learned of some drama that transpired at work regarding me and Skyy. Someone overheard Skyy discussing our issues at work and telling people I was too clingy and showed our text threads and call logs to other girls at work. I confronted Skyy about it. I told her that was the lowest thing she could do to discuss me with people I manage at work. I told her to clear my name. She apologized days after I brought it to her attention. Her apology felt genuine, she admitted to not meaning the things she said and had no reason, she just did it. I accepted her apology, but I still had an attitude about what she did in the first place. This transpired into another bigger situation at the job. She came up there angry to see me, but I was not at work. She stated that she wanted to fight me, and someone reported her. We both had to have a meeting at work. I did not think it should have escalated. Even though I was mad that things were happening back-to-back on the account of Skyy's dumb actions, we both produced a statement that would save both of our jobs and we were good.

By now, my 27th birthday was approaching. I planned a lingerie hotel party. I invited Skyy but we were not on good terms, so I didn't know if she was going to attend or not. The day before my party I received a text from her after not talking to her for two weeks that she purchased the plant that I liked. I told her again that I would like for her to come to my party. I invited Solar too, just in case she felt better with having him there with her. She agreed to come. We resumed normal conversations and caught up on the past few weeks. I kept flirting with Skyy and she flirted back with me. I was somewhat vocal that I wanted to fuck on my birthday. Some moments made me believe she was down, but some things she said gave me doubts. I would see how the night went and see what happens. Along with the plant, she got me a bedding set, a candle and a diffuser and oil set. I picked her up from her house and she rode with me to the party. My sister decorated the hotel room for me, and my guest started to arrive.

We both had to change clothes, so she got in the shower and invited me in with her. I got in. This was our first shower together. It felt special and I appreciated her for this unexpected, isolated, and intimate surprise. With the steam all around us and the water flowing on our naked bodies, I soaked in as much of her attention as I could before we had to return to the party. More than I wanted to make a move on her in the shower, I did not want to mess this sweet moment up. I resisted every bit of temptation to devour Skyy. My party was cool but not as exciting as I wanted it to be. My phone was dead so I had some guests who ended up leaving the hotel because they could not get to the room without me.

I tried to divide my attention between everyone at my party, but Skyy was my focus. I felt like she was a little uncomfortable, so I made extra attempts to make her as comfortable as possible. My judgement was probably impaired because I was under the influence again, but I thought I seen Skyy look upset, so I went over to her to see what was wrong and kissed her lips. Apparently, this was the wrong move because she got upset that I kissed her and didn't want to look like we were a couple. We proceeded to have a private conversation away from the party and she told me to entertain my guest who were present and not show her too much attention. I got a little more aggressive with my affection and Skyy didn't like it so she was ready to go home. She called Solar to come get her and left. The party was pretty much over because it was late and my mood shifted. When I did sober up I realized that I did do too much and made Skyy feel uncomfortable. Skyy stated that she wished she never came and that she wasn't attending the events the following day. I tried to talk to her and apologize but she wasn't feeling it.

This on and off pattern continued and became the foundation of how we operated the entire time of us knowing each other. There was always something that either one of us did that the other didn't like. When something happened, we couldn't work through so we stopped talking to each other, thinking that each time would be the last time but it wasn't. Sometimes Skyy would ask for us to be cool sometimes I would ask for things to go back to how they were. As long as we still worked at the same place we were expected to see each other at some point. We continued to cross paths for about a month at work and texted very little in between. The communication was very dry and minimal between us but we kept the door open. During our arguments Skyy used to say things like, "I'm happy with my man and I don't need you around." Each argument and break in between started to hurt a little more than the last one until I got used to them and started paying them less attention. When she and I were off, she and Solar appeared to be doing very well so I believed her each time that she said we were done.

Because I was so in tune with her emotionally, I could sense when something was wrong. I knew that if one of the three events that we talked about, engagement, marriage of pregnancy occurred that I would be crushed to the core. I've always felt like we were meant to be and will be together someday. I didn't know how we would get to that point, especially since we were so unstable but what I felt with her gave me a sense of forever when no one else has ever given me that feeling. I tracked her periods more than I tracked mine and accused her of being pregnant a few times. I think I was so scared of getting hurt in that way that I always tried to prepare myself that she was. I also felt like it was bound to happen because Solar knew that was the one thing he had above me- something that I as a woman, I could not do.

I don't know if I put it in the atmosphere too much and ended up manifesting it, or if I was having premonition. My thoughts were not erroneous assumptions. I arrived to work one day and noticed Skyy called out on an 8-hour shift- something that she never does. People already assumed I knew everything when it came to Skyy so I felt like I had to keep that persona up. I knew if I didn't say anything, they would. One coworker was giving me a report on the day and ended up saying, "We had a few call outs tonight, I'm sure you already know about Skyy." I didn't, but I just said yes because saying no would mean she would stop talking because she said too much or I would expose the fact that we weren't on good terms right now, and I didn't want anyone to know that either. Another day someone told me that she fainted at work and that they had to call for an ambulance. Hearing that really saddened my heart because I felt like I was supposed to be by her side and I wasn't. I started to feel guilty that we argued so badly in our last conversation and now I was blocked so I had no access to reach out to her.

I was at my job at the hospital the next day when my friend bombarded me with her phone. She wanted me to see Skyy's story on Instagram. By the look on her face, I already knew it was something serious and probably one of the three deal breakers. She posted that she was headed out of town for a well needed vacation with a pregnant woman emoji, and an expected due date in December. My pride would not let me show any real emotion. All of the puzzle pieces came together and this was just confirmation for me. I remember feeling really shocked and just blank-numb. I wasn't thrown off by Skyy being pregnant, I couldn't believe I just found out at work, on my friend's phone. I asked one thing of Skyy and out of everything else, this was the request that I cared about the most, to please have a conversation with me directly if this ever happened. As much as she knew I was worried this would happen, I thought I would be the first person to come to mind when it came to announcing the pregnancy.

I took it as a slap in the face because the people on her Instagram, in my eyes, were not even as close to her as I was. Some family some friends and a bunch of people she probably barely talks to was able to share that moment with her, and I still haven't heard it from her. Using the expected due date, I thought to calculate the conception date and see if she was pregnant during either of our birthdays or before that when I was asking her every month. Honestly if she was and didn't tell me the truth then, I didn't even want to know now. This was enough disappointment to digest. I calmed down, but I kept it no secret that I found out. I texted her and just in case I was blocked on her phone again, emailed her too saying "Congrats on your pregnancy!" She never responded but I was determined not to text anything in addition to that. I wouldn't express anything else that I thought or wanted to say about this pregnancy and the announcement until Skyy acknowledged me first. She expected a less calm reaction out of me, so to keep her on her toes, I had to give her the opposite.

In the meantime, I thought to myself what this meant for me. I played out different scenarios in my head as I tried to decipher the various possibilities. To the best of my ability, I weighed pros and cons, thought with my brain, and listened to my heart. There was a chance Skyy wouldn't want me present for good, due to our crazy history and I could either be happy or sad about her decision. I may have not wanted to deal with her because of the pregnancy and she could have been fine or not fine with my decision. What if I bonded with the baby and because I have no rights or shared biology, she takes the baby away from me? But what if I don't create a bond in the baby's early stages of life then Skyy and I reconnect in the future when the baby is older? I would feel like I missed out on important moments early on. I knew none of these answers. I knew this one thing, I really and truly loved Skyy, unconditionally!

The reality was that regardless of how and when the baby got here, the baby was the innocent soul in the equation. I couldn't stress Skyy too much with my emotions because pregnancy is delicate. It's really hard not to be happy for someone you love and I wanted to still be involved as her friend. Our work schedule showed that we were supposed to work together one weekend. I wanted to be prepared when we saw each other. If she tried to ignore me, I wanted to make it hard for her to do so. I made sure my hair was nice and flowy, my eyelashes were full, nails were pretty, I smelled delightful and my energy was charismatic. My plan worked.

I had to oversee the front end at the store. That was also the area where she worked. When I arrived she started the talk loud method. "I need a break. I need to drink some water. I'm starting to feel tired" she repeatedly said but not directly to anyone. I delegated someone to cover her and told her to take 10 minutes to rest. She smiled and took the break. When she came back she had a customer in her line who had a large bag of dog food. I saw it before she did. I told her to type the numbers to the barcode as I was calling them out. When she finished the item popped up on her screen. "Awwwww so you really do care about me." She said. "Of course I do." I responded back. "So you're not going to respond to my email?" I added. The whole time were talking, we were not really looking at each other because we were working at the same time so the dialogue was very undertone maybe even a little passive aggressive. She took a deep breath and said "Thank you", and walked away. When she got close to me again, I asked, "so it's true?" She confirmed that it was. "Did you plan it?" I interrogated. "Fuck no." She answered.

I started to feel slightly better that it was one of those things that just happened. It was neither planned nor prevented. "I cried when I saw the results and Solar was the first person I told. He didn't know I cried though. Then I told my family." She said. "Yea and you posted it on Instagram too. I told you I see everything. How come you didn't tell me Skyy?" I asked. "I really wanted to tell you, but we weren't on good terms and I just didn't know how to tell you. I didn't know how you would respond." She explained. "You just say it like you say everything else. Never worry what my response will be. So have you found a doctor yet?" I responded. From that moment on Skyy knew that she had me as her support. I could see the fear in her eyes disappear after we talked. She didn't owe me this explanation and vulnerability of her true feelings, but she was woman enough to give it to me and I appreciated that.

I decided to continue to rock with Skyy. We were friends too and friends don't let friends go through pregnancy alone. I would set aside my feelings and be present every step of the way. I believed if a baby was considered the worst thing that came out of everything we been through, then we were still doing good. I was there to wipe tears. I caught vomit with my hands. I learned her cravings and showed up with them before demand. We talked a lot of baby business and prayed together for a healthy baby, specifically a baby girl. We would be happy with either gender but she and I hoped for a girl, while Solar hoped for a boy. She had a beautiful, worriless pregnancy. Skyy stated that she did not want a boring pregnancy, so we had fun. We called it mommy fun. We bonded- she and I, She and Solar, and all three of us together. As a trio, we went bowling together, dinner at a lounge, White Waters, a Falcons game, the drive in movie theatre, and even carved pumpkins together for the Fall. When Solar and I had drinks Skyy would get mock tails or soft drinks made with a pretty garnish.

They had moments that called for them to prepare for the baby and as a family. We had mandatory girl time as we embraced this new life altering shift that was about to take place. Skyy included me in a lot of the preparation, so I did start to develop a bond with the baby during the pregnancy. Sex between Skyy and I resumed during the pregnancy and became more consistent than it was prior to. To her it was just for the sex. She wouldn't have sex with me if I was doing it because I loved her. She asked me each time if I did love her. Each time I lied straight through my teeth and told her that my feelings were gone, and that I wasn't still in love with her. If I wanted the sex to continue, that's what I had to do. I felt like I was betraying Solar just a tad bit because of how close we were all becoming as friends and, in a way, as family. I held on to this fear of my karma because I was really enjoying what Skyy and I was doing.

Although I wasn't upset with Skyy and I chose to be involved and was looking forward to being present for her. I still lived as the single woman that I was. Skyy was still with Solar and we had our superficial understanding. I still liked her in a deeper way but I learned to stop acting on those feeling for her because it brought about more chaos and confusion than peace. In a way, I was still waiting for Skyy. She did get pregnant but she didn't get engaged or married so there was still a chance for her and I to solidify something greater. I didn't press her about it. I did however, spin the block on one of my flings from my past. He wasn't too far in the archives though falling in line prior to Skyy. Sex with him was mediocre. I liked him a lot, loved him but I always felt like we were incompatible in the bedroom. I couldn't determine if the disconnect was coming from his performance or my lack of sexual interest in men. I needed to find out.

When I visited home, I went to see him and I tried to stay out of my head, let my hair down and just be present in the moment with him. It felt rushed to say the least. I couldn't even get in the head space I needed to get in to go there. I also knew what I felt with a female, and nothing I felt with her was remotely close to happening with him. Also, she called me while I was at his house and I couldn't ignore her call, so all of those factors put me out the mood. I would have to confess to Skyy about this encounter. I wouldn't volunteer the information immediately though but if she asked, I wouldn't lie to her. Another time, I went to a day party with one of my cousins. Skyy saw my story on IG and was complimenting me on how pretty I looked. She said that she was jealous because she wasn't there. She would do this anytime I was doing my own thing because she knew I would stop what I was doing to tend to her at any time. I tried to have a balance of my own life and her life just in case things between us got crazy again.

From the outside looking into her and Solar's dynamics, their relationship appeared to be taking a turn for the better. What I was seeing must have been wrong because Skyy texted me one morning asking if she could come live with me because her and Solar wasn't together anymore. I was so confused as to how they got to that point. I didn't ask for details. I just told her that I hope they wasn't both acting up while she was pregnant, and I told her that was fine if she moved in. Skyy wasn't asking to move in as a couple, she wanted to live with me as a friend. The more we talked about it though, the more I got excited and started to see it for something that it wasn't. Skyy asked to clear the air when she felt that I was a little too involved and excited about the baby. She told me that she's in a vulnerable space and that she didn't need me giving her the extra love and affection because it clouded her vision as that's not what she was asking for. I respected it. It was hard not expressing myself through romance and intimacy the way I always have, but I managed to resist it.

We spent a weekend together to allow her and Solar some space. I picked her up from home after work one night. When I arrived to her house, she had some of her things packed by the door. We discussed the plan earlier that day but I was sure that when it was time to execute the plan, that she would change her mind like she has before. She didn't change her mind. I helped her with her belongings and Solar pulled up as we were leaving. She told him that she would be leaving or a few days. He said ok. This was early in the first trimester, so she was constantly nauseous. When she got in the car she felt really sick and told me that she was experiencing pain. This was the first time that she rode with me while she was pregnant so I drove home with extra caution. I was now responsible for protecting an additional tiny life.

She moaned in agony most of the ride to my house. I told her if she didn't feel any better after laying down for an hour, then we would go to the Emergency Room. We arrived home and she tried to lay down but started crying. The hour wasn't up, but her tears were indicators that she wasn't able to rest. I got her back in the car and we headed to the hospital. My nerves were shot but I tried to be calm for Skyy. Due to Covid regulations, I could not be with her during her visit. I begged the receptionist to make me an exception to the rule, but she didn't budge. I helped her check in, waited by her side until they called her back, but had to leave when she left.

I bawled as I paced the outside of the hospital back and forth. When she called me from the room, I stopped crying just enough to listen to the doctor in the background. Everything was fine with her. Skyy was just experiencing pregnancy and everything that came with it- times two! The moment that I lost when Skyy announced her pregnancy was just restored with something even greater. I was now the first to know that she was carrying multiples! The ride back home was better. I was calmer, she was too. We talked and laughed. The way this aligned so quickly in my favor was surreal.

When we got back home she asked for a snack but fell asleep by the time I made it for her. I had to work the next morning but end up only working a half day so I could be home with Skyy. We went out for ice cream at Jeni's, got some food, and came back home. The next day we shopped at Target for two of every baby gadgets and attended her sister's field day themed birthday party at Piedmont Park. I met a lot of her family and we had a great time. Knowing what we had been through, I took in every moment that I possibly could with her and thought of our time as a deeper bonding opportunity. She ended our weekend together with a surprise picnic in the park for us. She purchased a blanket, a cooler, and snacks and I drove us to a park where she set everything up for us so nicely. To me this was intimacy. It was a well thought out, simple, way for us to isolate ourselves together and just be happy. We didn't talk about relationship and romance, but because the energy was so deep, it just came out without either one of us trying. It's beautiful to see and even more beautiful to experience but fighting it creates so much turmoil internally and I believe that played a role in our instability.

We fell out again because she felt like I was getting too attached and we didn't talk for months. The truth was that her and Solar decided to work out the kinks in their relationship and she decided to stay home with him rather than live with me. I would have been fine with her telling me that, instead she had to find something to make me the cause of her changing her mind. Everything we purchased for the babies and left at my house, she made me bring it to her house. Sadly, I made the decision that my involvement with her and the twins would no longer be in my best interest.

After that, I started to date. I got out of my commitment bag and got into my hoe bag. Because, who? My tolerance with Skyy's bullshit became lower each time she got an attitude about something. I knew that someone would appreciate the qualities I have that Skyy took for granted and that I could dodge the drama and somewhat reset with a new person. The universe seemed to agree because one day while I was taking a walk in my neighborhood, I crossed paths with a girl who was just too attractive not to acknowledge. She was pretty. She had braces, tattoos, piercings, and pretty hair. I liked how she talked and the perfect mixture of hood and class her vibe gave off. We exchanged numbers and conversed a little. She entered my life as the perfect Ray of

Sunshine, very understanding of the on/off situation with Skyy. Instead of forcing me to be something more concrete with her, she met me where I was. She was honest with what she could offer me and that was this- to fill a void so that I wouldn't feel the need to keep running back to Skyy. She and I made the agreement that she would be that person for me. She would be there when I needed conversation, time, sex or whatever. She promised me the first time we had sex that it would be all for me. She wanted me to solely enjoy without focusing on reciprocating.

When the time presented itself for her to deliver, she did just that. Gracefully and with the upmost level of self-assurance, she stamped her name on my clit with so much gratitude. This human radiance had a touch so sensual and a tongue so enduring. Whatever cloud Skyy took me on, Radiance took me higher. I was sure to keep her locked in, close by, and within reach. I reciprocated with random acts of service, cash apps, gifts, food -trick shit. We had some special moments together too. She liked when I cooked shrimp tacos. Around Christmas time we decorated the tree at her house. When I was sick, she brought tea, ginger ale and Pedialyte for me. We visited the haunted house for Halloween, and as a bonus, she kept my hair done so pretty! We lasted for a year before I fumbled the ball with her. The inconsistency amongst us clouded my judgement which caused me to make one bad decision that would be enough to lose all of her trust.

In true Skyy fashion, any signs of me moving on just didn't sit right with her. Of course she would come insert her ass back in the middle of what I have going on now, demanding some type of pick up where we left off kind of respect from me. She approached me one day at work out of nowhere and just said, "It's girls. Our prayers were answered" I congratulated her. She must have expected more out of me because she came to my area where I was detailing product on the shelves and rearranged everything that I completed. When I asked her why was she doing that she said because I was ignoring her. I explained to her that she seemed pretty sure that she wouldn't be talking to me again and that I never expected for her to share any more news with me about the babies. I appreciated it, but it wasn't something I could just jump back into, as I had adjusted to the distance. She explained to me that she wanted to clear the bad blood between us and that she did want me a part of the twins' life. I told her that I was hesitant because the up and down patterns continued. When she initially discussed the baby shower with me, I told her that I wasn't sure if I should attend. I started to resist her efforts to amend anything. She kept acting sad about my decisions which caused me to rethink if I was being too hard or mean towards her. She knew that her being pregnant meant she could just about have everything her way. Even though I help start that mindset I didn't want to keep it up because of how she abused it.

To make it up to me, Skyy started to reciprocate the energy I was putting out in the way that I was there for her. She split her food stamps and her WIC in half with me and went grocery shopping for her house and mine. When I needed her to go get a money order for me to turn in for my bigger apartment, she got on the train after one of her doctor's appointments and purchased the money order for me while I was at work. After I moved she even helped me assemble my bed back together, all while pregnant. My apartment was still empty as I did not purchase furniture immediately. Skyy's sister was throwing away a glass table that Skyy thought would be perfect for my apartment. Personally, I already had a vision of how I wanted my apartment set up. I was adamant on all new purchases, no consigned furniture but since it was a gift from Skyy I accepted it for sentimental purposes. The table was just as unstable as us because I sold it the moment we had another argument. I didn't expect Skyy to find out but she came inside my apartment after a night of hanging out to find the space where the table used to be empty.

I put my pride aside and I continued my involvement and being present for her. Skyy gave birth to 2 beautiful baby girls, who were both the perfect mixture of her and Solar. I stayed beside Skyy every step of the way, continuing the bond with the twins that started from the womb.

As a push gift I took Skyy to the spa for us to enjoy a luxury manicure and pedicure. We all spent Christmas 2021 and New Year's 2022 together. That year on her birthday, Solar expressed that he wanted me to bring a plus one because he didn't like hanging out as a trio. I interpreted that as he got tired of me being around and suggested that they go out as a couple and I would celebrate her birthday with her as her friend. To make sure I wasn't stuck in the house while she was out having fun, I scheduled to go to the strip club with my friends on her birthday. I still delivered her gift to her at midnight but we talked and she expressed how she would never forgive me for not celebrating her birthday with her so I cancelled my plans with my friends and attended her birthday.

To keep everyone happy I invited a plus one. When my birthday came after her though, I didn't like how Skyy didn't consider my special day for me. She told me she would send a gift to my house and that she couldn't attend my party due to having to save money. My argument was that she really didn't need money to attend my party because I would cover for her and also quality time, which is what I really wanted more than anything cost no money. Me expressing my strong feelings about my birthday turned into her not liking that I wasn't understanding so she didn't want to talk to me after that. I got tired of talking and expressing myself to someone who never heard of understood me so I started reciprocating the same energy. I had built up resentment in me for Skyy over the years and instead of suppressing it I let it out. On Mother's Day, I didn't acknowledge it for her. When she noticed and told me that it hurt her feelings, I reminded her of when mine was hurt. It hurt me to do this to her, but I had to care about me more. It started to look like Skyy was dragging me along and putting a friend title on us just to keep me around.

As more time passed, we were now approaching our 2-year mark, I started to reflect on how this all started and where this was headed. Skyy either wanted me or she didn't. She either wanted Solar or she didn't. If she didn't make the decision, then I would have to. I was approaching my prime and I had to put somethings in perspective. With everything that I have put into this with Skyy, I still had no ring, no title, no respect and no freedom. I may have done too good of a job suppressing my romantic feelings for Skyy because I played the friends role really well. It made her comfortable but it had me confused. This conversation was always so sensitive though. If I started the conversation, I could risk Skyy not wanting to be friends again. I couldn't keep allowing her to think I didn't still like her in that way though. I needed to know what was up and what was her plans regarding me and Solar before I moved on with my life on a deeper level with someone. Each time I tried to initiate the talk, I froze up and couldn't move forward with bringing the subject up.

Somewhere around this time I thought of this brilliant business idea that I did try out and do well solo, but believed it would have taken off better with Skyy. I tested out the idea of Only Fans. I had to get as creative as possible to create as many streams of income that I could, as fast as I could, with less work. The men who flooded my DMs each time I posted something sexy would now be my clients. From my close friends list, which consisted of followers 21 years of age, people would send me a fee to enjoy sexy and sensual content that I create. Sometimes I would create in sexy lingerie, other times I created absolutely naked in the shower. It was fun while it lasted, but it upset Skyy every time I did it. I really only wanted to move forward with Skyy behind the camera with me, but was too scared to pitch the idea to her.

Skyy and I had an impromptu car date one night. This consisted of us just sitting in the car with some wine, music and deep conversation. She initiated the conversation, so it made things a little easier. She asked me if I was still in love with her. I told her that I loved her but there were times I fell in and out of love with her. She expressed that she wanted to explore sexually outside of Solar but she didn't know with who. She had other male options but she also had my feelings to consider. I asked her about her plans for us. I told her that I reconsidered the poly relationship long ago and I was comfortable with it now. She didn't rule it out. Instead she asked questions for clarity and asked me if I was sure. I told her with communication we would all write our own rules. Either the three of us could be in a relationship together, or she could have two separate relationships- one with Solar and one with me. Since we been through so much together it only made sense. We were basically already living the poly life in a way we could just define our dynamics even more. I expressed that I believe the reason for our roller coaster dynamics was because of both of us fighting our feelings for each other and that my attitude towards her could be a little lighter and not so tense if we were honest about what we wanted and tried it out. I told Skyy with the way she manipulates and gets her way, if she wanted this to happen she knew how to make it happen.

She had the best of both worlds already. Solar would give her the world if she asked and I would too. I never known anyone who had this luxury of having two people so into them like Skyy did. Skyy told me that she would talk it over with Solar and let me know. I felt so much hope. I just knew once Solar knew I was on board; he would try it out for Skyy. I don't know how Skyy presented it to him, because I wasn't there but he didn't agree with it. To him he already had his family and it wasn't a good look. I didn't like nor understand it but I respected it. I started to picture my future without Skyy. When the twins turned 1 Skyy had an attitude with me at the time so I missed their first birthday party because of that. My twenties were almost up. I had a few more goals to accomplish before I was ready to start a family of my own. I talked to my old fling, who is a great father to his son about everything.

It took me a few conversations to get him on board but he became open to trying to have a baby with me.

8 "911, location of emergency?"

This was perfect! I wanted a baby and I wanted my baby to have two parents. I didn't care if my baby had 2 moms or a mom and dad, as long as we co parented well together. If the second parent was a dad though, there was a possibility I wouldn't want the relationship aspect, just the parenting. I tracked my ovulation and Old Fling and I planned conception for August 2023. With only 7 more months until my 30th birthday, the timing worked perfectly for me. I wasn't sure how Skyy would feel nor did I care because this was about me. Again, I wouldn't volunteer the information, but if she asked, I would tell her. I didn't see growth between Skyy and I, so I started counting the idea of us out to save myself the disappointment. Words didn't match actions and I wasn't about begging someone to make something official with me. Her involvement with my baby would be great, but if she didn't want to I would be fine as well.

The conversation came up one day when I was spending time with Skyy and the twins. She watched how I interacted with them and told me I would be a great mom one day. I told her that I hoped so as that was my goal and I was ready. We talked about how the twins may react to me having a baby of my own. I reassured her that the twins will always have their place in my life and that they wouldn't feel any less love. She knew I would be open to children once I turned 30. She wasn't aware that now, I wanted to conceive naturally and that I would be starting the process prior to me turning 30. When we previously spoke on this subject, I mentioned artificial insemination and IVF as possible methods of conception for me. I changed my mind from IVF being my primary method to being my last resort. We were considered "on" during this time frame. That meant we just recovered from an "off". I was careful with my words, not to say too much but her questions were specific. Not only did I have to tell Skyy that I was actively planning for pregnancy, but I had a recent hook up with someone new. I managed to keep the answers vague yet truthful in this moment.

The new girl was my fun girl. Her energy was fresh, and she had more of an exotic vibe. She was so great at dancing and modeling that she did it for a living. She had the tightest grip on my attention and could accommodate my spontaneity well. I loved her hustle, it came natural to her. She had the look and the body for the entertainment industry. She was the lifelong fantasy that came true! What was crazy is that I really grew up knowing Fun Girl from 229, so our first interaction as adults was more like a reconnection.

I wear my emotions on my sleeve so there is not much I can get pass Skyy. I don't like withholding information from her because I don't like her withholding information from me. But also because it wears me down and she ends up discerning that something is wrong anyways. She would be more upset finding out something later when there was an opportunity for me to acknowledge something sooner and I chose not to. That's exactly how this encounter took place. Skyy and I went to Cascade's adult skate session one night after midnight. Usually when we spend time together, I'm happy and relaxed because I'm with my favorite human in the world. I was happy to see her but the guilt in me felt so heavy that I couldn't even enjoy myself. I couldn't even fake it. She kept asking me what was up and encouraging me to talk but every time I tried to, I got stuck. We were doing so good and I just didn't want to switch the vibe. It was important though and more than anything she deserved the truth. I told Skyy that we needed to talk and that I had two things to tell her. My plan was to come clean, get this weight off my heart and tell her about my encounter with fun girl and pregnancy plans. After seeing the disappointing hurt look in her eyes when I told her about Fun Girl, I just couldn't go on to the next subject.

We spent 4th of July weekend with my parents who came to visit in Atlanta. Skyy was still upset with me. In an insinuating manner, she asked my dad if he met my "girlfriend". He told her that he assumed it was her as she was the only person he met. She continued to give me the cold shoulder to keep me thinking. Everything that I thought would happen after she found this out didn't happen, but everything that I never expected, did happen. Skyy's actions towards me changed in the weirdest way. Instead of becoming distant, she drew closer to me. She hinted at moving out from with Solar and moving in with me. We revisited the possibility of us trying to work out an official relationship. We even had sex again, really good, selfless, passionate sex that I could admit to loving her to.

I discussed how happy I would be if we worked out. I voiced my fears as well. If we rushed it and one of us messed it up, we could risk our relationship and friendship for good. Also, if I got used to her being around, I would feel hurt if she ended up leaving. I was torn. It wasn't worth losing everything over, but it was worth trying out to see. We discussed goals together and made plans on how we would achieve them. She agreed to having a baby together, because she didn't like how my plan excluded her. She also wanted me to know that she was still sexually attracted to men which led me to ask her if she was seeing or considering anyone else besides me. She stated that she wasn't. Now since we were working towards something that I wanted for the longest, I would put my solid pregnancy plans on hold and Skyy and I would take things slow. At the end of the year, we would decide if we were merging our lives together under one roof as girlfriends with the hopes of becoming wives and parents. If we lasted, we would spend Christmas together in matching pajamas.

This shit should have felt as wrong as 1+1=3. She wasn't even out of the house that her and Solar shared together. She recently told me not too long ago that she didn't see me beyond a friend. We couldn't communicate effectively. We both resented each other from things of the past that we never really healed from, only swept under the rug. In the past, some verbal arguments became physical. But when she told me that if we focused on the past then we would never have a future, I melted into her arms. It's like she was making Solar jealous, by flaunting me around him. He started to hate me because he already felt like I was taking Skyy from him, so every time he seen me I could imagine it triggered more anger. I told Skyy that I would feel better if I asked for Solar's blessing to have her and she told me that I didn't need it and what she says goes. Not only were we having amazing sex, but some of our sexual encounters took place in their bedroom, while Solar was at work.

Skyy switched up our plans. She didn't wait until the end of the year to move in. I noticed she used present tense when discussing and not future tense. I didn't address it though. I didn't want her to feel like I never wanted her to move in, I just wanted us to take our time. I told Skyy I wanted her to focus on paying her car off and once it was paid she can assist with paying something towards the rent. We wouldn't split bills in half because our income wasn't the same. She agreed and after about three days of moving, we cohabited. Skyy kept the twins during the day, and Solar at night so the twins came with her too. It was a beautiful chaos. Each day became a little more normal. Skyy and Solar tried out different pick up and drop off schedules, but the schedule wasn't allowing Skyy time to rest during the day since she worked at night. I told Skyy I would tend to the twins in the morning until I left home to work 2nd shift at the hospital so that she could get some rest. Some mornings it was easier for her to keep the twins at Solar's house and just stay at his place until he got off of work. When my schedule allowed me to, I would drive to his house to be with her. I traded my sleep until noon mornings for 7am drop offs, Disney Channel, breakfast for twins, breakfast in bed for Skyy, and diaper changes, all with the hopes of having the twins sleep before I leave home. Sometimes it was seamless, sometimes it wasn't. Adjusting to my new life wasn't bad at all, I loved it. Skyy and the twins added so much value to my life and I was a happier person overall.

Skyy was my empress, and she received the red-carpet royal treatment from me. I warmed blankets and towels for her every morning since she worked in below freezing temperatures. I took my time massaging her, packed her lunch, went to see her at work on her break, and did everything in my power to express my love to her. She attended to my emotional needs very well. When she spoke on our future goals together, that gave me reassurance. We spent as much time as we could together. When there were disagreements, she initiated talking things over. On her off days she waited on me to get home for us to shower together and the sex was passionate! She was still Skyy, but I had never experienced this Skyy before. My love for her grew each day. I didn't want us to get so comfortable living together that we forgot to date each other. I also wanted to plan an official celebration for us by asking Skyy to be my girlfriend. I purchased balloons, LED lights, roses, teddy bears, and candles and set a date for my friends to come help me decorate the house while Skyy was dropping the twins off to Solar. I told Skyy to reserve the day for us, because I had something special planned.

I always felt like Skyy had a secret agenda that she was plotting. Her telling me that she was still attracted to men was her way of telling me that she wanted to be involved with a man sexually while we were together. She explained her need for penetration. She wanted me to be involved with him as well since I wanted to carry the baby. If we both chose the guy, I wouldn't have had a problem with it but Skyy was introducing me to men she just met who liked her. Her choice of men was not the type of men I wanted to be involved with, let alone get pregnant by. She went outside of me and asked one of her coworkers if he would have a baby with us and he said yes. She told him to have a date with us but planned it on the same day I planned the girlfriend proposal for her.

My issue with the men she wanted to bring was that she was connecting with them before they ever met me. Another reason was that Skyy barely knew them and honestly, I just couldn't trust Skyy's judgement. Her issue with the men I suggested was the same. I asked Skyy if she liked her coworker, and she told me know. When I saw how they interacted with each other I could see they liked each other. I asked her to call the date off with him because when they were texting he asked her to send him pictures of her, and was calling her pretty and telling her that he wished he could have her. She sent him pictures of her face then he requested pictures of her feet, specifically soles crossed. For him to feel comfortable talking to her that way meant she entertained if before. I felt like Skyy's feet were my intimate spot. When I told Skyy how I felt about him she told me that she no longer wanted to have a baby with me and that I was too emotional.

Her actions sparked a lot of curiosity within me. She was watering down the truth or leaving out some details. Understand that I watched how she handled me when she was with Solar and I became familiar to Skyy's antics over time. She wanted to make me jealous so I could react. Once I reacted, she would tell me I'm the problem by being too emotional which will cause me to self-reflect and start to believe that she is right. I would then feel bad and give in to become understanding because "I love her unconditionally." I started crying and she caressed and comforted me. Then she took my hand and guided me to our bedroom and started kissing me and taking off my clothes. I laid there while she went in our closet and got some toys. We had a few of them, and I could tell her motive by which ones she selected.

She used the whip and butt plug to punish me. She turned me on all fours and as hard as she could hit me with the whip. She told me that she has always considered my wants and feelings and that now I wasn't considering hers. Then she took the butt plug with no lube and tried to insert it in me forcefully but I clinched and moved so she couldn't. My body language was saying no and I asked her to stop. This felt violating. This was not her genuinely fantasizing a dominant moment, Skyy was abusing me, misusing sex as a way to have power over me. In my mind I thought that this was only going to get worst because this was not the first time.

I pushed her off of me and went to the bathroom to clean myself up. My body was sore. Skyy left her phone in the bathroom and against my better judgement I looked through her text messages with her coworker. She told him that she didn't want to focus on the arrangement she just wanted to focus on her enjoying her time getting to know him because she was starting to like him. He texted her for rides to and from work and they got coffee before work every day. I snapped. I rushed out the bathroom and attacked Skyy. She was standing up and I grabbed her and threw her on the bed hitting her and yelling to her that she's a liar. We tussled as she tried to get me off her. She contained my hands and told me I was reading everything wrong and that she was talking about focusing on the relationship between me and her the whole time. Then hit me in the face and grabbed her things for work. I got in the shower and she came in the bathroom and said that I never had to worry about her again then stormed out of the house.

I snapped out and realized what I had done and felt horrible. I jumped out the shower didn't dry off, just threw on some clothes to run behind her. When I got to the car she drove off. I panicked. If something happened to Skyy on the way to work and this was my last interaction with her I would never forgive myself. I couldn't believe that I lost my composure right along with her. I was supposed to be the strong one. My cry was more like a wail. I could feel my heart becoming empty. This sounds crazy but leaving wasn't an option. I was determined that we were going to work it out. The only thing I could do was call my best friend. Skyy texted me and said that she loved me with her whole heart and asked if we could start fresh and never hit each other again. I agreed. That night I filled the whole house in the decorations as my apology so she could see when she came home the next morning.

I never did the proposal. In the same week there was another guy who Skyy said wanted to take her to the movies. I asked her what time was she leaving and she told me that I was going with her. I asked her to fill me in on the conversation between her and the guy and he wasn't taking her to the movies he wanted us to come to his house. She told him that we were down to fuck him. I didn't want to go but I told Skyy to do her thing. I started talking to her like we were just friends because that's what she was acting like. Skyy laid on top of me and put all her weight on me until I felt suffocated. I was so angry that she kept trying to hurt me. Using a firm tone, I asked her to get off me and she didn't. I tried to push her off of me but the grip only got tighter. She told me if I kept moving that she would stay there so I stopped. I told her if she's going to react this way when she gets upset, then she would have to leave. She stayed home that night and it took everything in me not to get my lick back in her sleep. It was evident that Skyy was getting me back from old things that I've done. I could tell the difference in someone fighting out of anger, but this felt like pure hate. I don't think Sky cared if she really hurt me when she fought me. That made me angry because I could never bring myself to genuinely wanting to physically hurt her.

Each time I didn't address her actions when she got physical, it indicated that I still had a tolerance for it. Skyy didn't come home after work one morning. Usually I would call but I got tired of telling Skyy about my abandonment issues and how her not coming home makes me feel emotionally so I acted like I didn't notice. She called me and my attitude was nonchalant. She told me that she liked another person and that she wasn't trying to make it a shared arrangement. She added that she wants to carry a baby of her own because if I had a baby it wouldn't feel like the baby is the twin's siblings. This upset me because I never saw or treated the twins as anything less. She suggested that she move out the house and I told her to do whatever she thought was best. Skyy was acting like she was single so I did too. I resumed conversations with multiple people. I went to work and Skyy went to our house later. I put the hand warmers that I purchased for her in my car since she had enough men, she was dealing with who could give her some hand warmers. She didn't go to work. She asked me to come home early but I didn't. We were talking on the phone, and I knew she was mad and she was saying that she couldn't wait for me to get home so we could "discuss" our issues. I could tell by the sarcasm in her voice that she was trying to fight.

When I got off I let her know that I was on my way home. Her car wasn't there when I pulled up so I figured she wouldn't be coming home as a way to get back at me. I went inside our house and there was a bouquet of mixed flowers on the mantle for me. I laughed because they weren't roses which are my favorite. I got in the shower and locked the door. Skyy came in the house banging on the door with black gloves on. I asked her why she had gloves on. She said so that her fingerprints would be on any evidence. She also told me that she had already taken my phone and my keys. She went through my messages and seen that I was entertaining people too. She started getting in my face, so I pushed her back. Then she started hitting me, so I started hitting her.

We fought all over the house and neither of us planned on stopping. I blacked out again so I don't remember much. She went to the kitchen and got a knife and was waving it around me. She choked me, so I had to bite her arm to loosen her grip. She got a hand full of my braids and with the other hand began to cut my hair at the root with the knife. I heard her say, "This is what you care about the most." I was trying to keep the knife from cutting me not knowing that she already did. I felt a cool sensation down my arm so I lifted it and I had bright red blood dripping down my arm from a cut on my wrist. I looked over on the bed and the blood stained the comforter. I didn't feel it but I could see it. The cut was deep and I could see the ridges in my skin from the knife.

I panicked. I tried to explain to Skyy that the twins sleep in this bed and on the comforter and now bad energies was on the bed. She said that we could wash the comforter and everything would be fine. I told her that there was no way that she loved me. She told me that she did and that was the only reason why she fought me. I didn't feel any love from her. I felt like I invested more love than her. I remembered my recent decline to her request for her to pee in my mouth. The first thing I thought when she asked me that was that she was trying to have some soul tie on me that kept me connected to her. I asked her what she gets out of me drinking her urine and she told me it gives her power over me.

To make an even request, I told her to lick the blood that was coming from my wrist. She was the reason I was bleeding and I already felt like she had me stuck under some love spell because I felt like I couldn't leave her. If this was true, then I wasn't about to be the only one stuck. She licked it and swallowed it and held her tongue out showing me that it was all gone. I don't know why but that was so satisfying to watch. Even if it was meaningless, it proved something to me. I believed that she loved me, and I looked passed her abusive ways. I was still upset, but there was room to reconcile. She asked me to get in the shower with her and I didn't want to. When she told me that she would give my phone back, I got in with her. This shower wasn't relaxing it was painful. We finished the shower and she gave me my phone.

That night she held me and started crying. She apologized to me and told me that she really did enjoy being with me, she just didn't want us to smoother each other from always being glued at the hip. She explained her reason for wanting to choose a male for us was because she wanted to make sure that she liked him enough to have a sexual connection with. We got out the shower and she wrapped my scars in bandages. Love blinded me and I forgave her for everything. She said that she didn't want to wait any longer and that she wanted us to start our relationship, so she asked me to be her girlfriend and I said yes!

I returned to work the next day like nothing ever happened. When people addressed my bandages, I lied to cover up what really happened to me. To protect Skyy and to save myself the embarrassment, I never mentioned this to anyone. I disappointed myself by letting our dynamics get too far. I felt like a failure and like I disappointed everyone who loved me. I stripped my dad of his desire to protect me. I shielded my friends from supporting me. Domestic abuse was always one of those things that I heard about happening to other people. Never did I imagine that I would experience it firsthand, especially from someone I was deeply in love with. Being strong in any other area was never a problem-my career, my accomplishments, my social life but when it came down to me, this girl, and this relationship I couldn't be strong for myself.

We planned a vacation to get a break from reality and get our relationship back on track. Solar really didn't want us to go. He gave us a hard time regarding childcare that caused us to cancel the first trip we planned. We rescheduled for a different day, but I ended up finding more text messages in her phone. I needed a break from Skyy. Instead of cancelling our trip I called Fun Girl to go for a ride along with me. She was able to go so we planned for her to stay over at the house while Skyy was at work. If we left the house before Skyy returned, we would be good. We went to Hilton Head to spend a day at a hotel resort, and I came back the next day. Of course, Skyy did something to try to top what I was doing.

I really wasn't trying to make Skyy feel away, I simply just needed a mental break. Fun Girl and I respected my relationship and didn't have sex on the trip, I just needed someone with me for safety purposes. I plotted a plan that would give me insight on how Skyy really felt if I had a baby outside of her. She acted like she didn't care, but when I spoke on still going through with it she got upset. I used a friend's positive pregnancy test and left it for Skyy to see as if it were mine. She cried and said that she couldn't believe I went outside of her and excluded her from my journey. I told her it wasn't mine. For her that was the last straw because it was such a sensitive subject that I played around with. I understood her, however; I felt the need to show her what reality could be if I did move forward with my original plan.

We began to discuss separation more. I suggested separation often since Skyy no longer wanted the relationship. Continuing to live together was a benefit for her and I would just feel like she was using me even more. If she was going to move on like she had already started doing, then she needed to do that outside of the house that I shared with her. I walked in on her cuddled with another coworker watching a movie in the living room. She told me that she was inviting multiple over for a movie night and to my understanding both guys were gay ad liked each other. Only one was there and they were watching a movie together.

The next day she told me that she was going to door dash on our shared account and left me home with the twins. She was gone for hours, and I never saw an order come through. When I called and texted her, she didn't answer. I started to worry about her but when I knew that she was ok I got mad. She lied about where she was going, and she didn't answer my phone calls knowing I was at home with two babies. The twins were fine, I got them both to go to sleep but my calls should never have been ignored.

When Skyy returned home she didn't see anything wrong with what she did. I started putting her things by the door. She went back and forth with me and told me she wasn't leaving. Someone was though- I stopped packing her things then packed my things to get away from the house again. I felt like everything that I built was slipping out of the palms of my hands. I sat back and just looked at the twins, at Skyy and thought about how they really became my family. My life was about to take a devastating turn. Skyy took the speaker and played music to communicate with me. I heard the lyrics to K Michelle's *Cry* for the first time. Skyy watched me as the song played and our eyes met when the chorus played. She was dead serious. That's exactly what she wanted me to do. I changed my mind. I told her that I really didn't want her to leave, but it felt like she was going to eventually leave anyways. She told me to put her things back in the closet and we agreed to spend the weekend together. I went as far as printing out a marriage application, filling out my portion and posting the paper on our refrigerator as "goals". If we worked out and she decided to fill out her side, then we would do it. She only took it down and told me to put it away when she saw it.

9 uno, uno out!

After one too many fights, lonely nights, and watching Skyy plot her best life around the idea that no matter what, I will stick around, I started to develop even more anger, rage and resentment towards her. We had separated for an entire weekend. I returned to work on Monday and ended up seeing a flier for Tamar Braxton's upcoming 10-year Love and War Tour in which she was looking for dancers. I sent the flier to Skyy as I know for a fact she is one of the most talented dancers I know, and I thought it would be an amazing opportunity for her.

She said thank you and about an hour later I gave her a call to check in on her and tell her to be safe going to work. She answered, and we shared that we both had a good weekend and even discussed a tentative plan to start packing to move into our two-bedroom apartment as the idea of our continuing to live together was still on the table. She told me that she wasn't going to work; instead, she was going to the drive-in movie theater with the same coworker from the previous night.

I questioned if her work schedule had changed. It didn't. She voluntarily called out of work but couldn't do the same when it was time for us to spend time together because apparently there had been prior counsels with her time and attendance at work. She told me he was coming to the house to pick her up. I said OK and continued to work. While at work thoughts started to flood my brain. I noticed that talking to her and attempting to be cordial with her only confused me more. I felt the division and tension between us no matter how cool we tried to be. I shared my feelings with her through a text, never got a response, and headed home after my shift.

When I arrived home, I noticed a box of Trojan condoms on top of the valet trash can we kept outside. I proceeded to enter my apartment, and there was a glass bong on the coffee table where they smoked. The LED candles I used to decorate the house in a romantic setting for her were put away, but some of them were powered on as if she had them all on but didn't properly turn them all off. I walked to the bedroom to find a pair of thongs on the floor at the end of the bed. The bed remained made. The fact that Skyy and I did have sex in her and Solar's house at the end of their relationship gave me no belief that Skyy would spare my feelings in my house at the end of our relationship. To me, this was just another scheme she had plotted towards me, rather for a reaction or revenge.

I sent Skyy another text telling her this was the last straw and she had to go. "You, the condom box in the trash can, my red candles, and your panties on the floor. All of you must go! By the way, you and he (referring to her co-worker/new boo at this point) have a surprise waiting outside when you return," I texted.

Soon after I hit send, I took the bong and threw it outside, breaking it on the concrete as I wanted that to be the very first thing they noticed when they tried to come back. Since I came home to a disturbing surprise, so would she, was the logic behind my thought process.

She called me. "Did you put my things outside, Starr?" she asked, calmly, but with a slight panic in her voice.

"No, I didn't put your things outside." I responded in a calm but sarcastic tone.

"So, what's the surprise you're talking about?" she continued to inquire.

"You will see," I finished.

"I'm having a good day, but I will fight you and not spare you if you threw my things outside," she added.

I thought ahead on how this whole night could turn out, so I was proactive in preparing myself as I am well familiar with Skyy's patterns and antics by now. I knew that in return, Skyy could return home extremely angry and another fight could occur. I moved the loveseat closer to the door so that when she unlocked the door she couldn't rush in the house just in case she was angry. I also took all of the knives out of the kitchen because we would never repeat an episode to that extent again. I tucked my keys under my pillow and kept my phone close by me so that she could not take it.

Not too much time had passed before Skyy texted me to open the gate. Then she called me again. "What?" I answered.

"Will there be any problems if we come eat our food in the house?" she asked.

If there is anything Skyy knows how to do and do very well is push me to a higher level of pissed-the-fuck-off more than what I already was. I was a week away from payroll with an over drafted account because of taking care of house responsibilities and looking out for Skyy until she got paid, but when she got paid she resumed thinking about herself. I also repeatedly requested that Skyy do her moving on far away from where we live and where I can't see. I find it extremely disrespectful for either of us to flaunt the next person around the other. I didn't do it to her, even when I had a right to before we made things official, and I didn't want it done to me. She didn't honor that request, but again, I couldn't be surprised because Solar requested the same thing towards me during and even before the transition, and she didn't honor his request either. She purposely had me in his space just to make him even more upset and she was doing the same to me.

"Absolutely, there will be major problems if you two come eat your food in the house. Why can't y'all go eat where he lives?" I know what I have provided and contributed to Skyy's life, so anyone who wanted her next should be able to do the same thing or more for her.

"Did you have sex in my house Skyy?" I asked her with a tone indicating that I have zero tolerance remaining for her.

"First of all, we live together, so it's our house, so stop saying just your house. And no, we did not have sex. It's an old condom box." She attempted to reassure me, but I still don't believe it to be true today. The first thing she was supposed to do when she got paid is have my back like I had hers. Also, the free time she had to spend with someone else was time I felt was stolen from our spending time together. Up until we started living together, we would spend so much quality time. I always made sure our home and everyone in it was taken care of before I spent an extra dime or shifted my time elsewhere. My anger came from Skyy not reciprocating the same energy when I depended on her.

She entered the house and apparently didn't notice the bong on the concrete outside because she didn't acknowledge it up front. She attempted to come into the bedroom, which I had locked, so she started knocking on the door. I opened it.

"So we can't come in the house?" she asked again in a more challenging manner as if my answer would change now that we are face to face.

"No, go to his house. I asked that you not do that around here," I responded.

"Well, how do you expect us to move into a bigger home together if we have tension now?" she asked.

"I don't want to continue living with you," I told her again. This time makes about my fifth time saying that I didn't want us to live together anymore. "Skyy, if we are not going to be together and work towards being back together, there is no need for us to live together. Besides, I don't think it's safe," I told her again.

"Why are there knives in the room?" she asked me.

"Isn't hiding knives something that you do? "I responded.

She left the room while stating to cancel the new apartment. Shortly after she left she came back. My adrenaline began to rush. This felt familiar. Although I am very angry, I really don't feel like going through another one of these episodes tonight.

"Starr, where is the bong? Because I don't see it in the living room where we left it," she added.

"It's outside broken on the concrete; I threw it out," I responded.

"Why would you do that?" she asked. In disbelief, she went outside to go see for herself because I guess she thought I was lying.

She went back to where he was waiting in her car, and I'm assuming told him what happened to his bong and asked him how much it cost because when she came back inside she told me that I needed to send him $16.00 to replace it.

"I'm not sending him anything. He disrespected my house, so I disrespected his belongings." I told her.

"He never disrespected your house. We never fucked in the house. He didn't touch anything that was yours, and Starr, we are not together, so you don't control what I do," she argued. "So send the money," she added.

"I don't have it," I told her in all honesty.

"Let me see," she said as she started grabbing for my phone and pinning me down.

"So you're really about to take some money from me and fight me over this nigga?" I asked her while looking directly into her almond shaped eyes.

"I'm not fighting you over him. I'm fighting you because you're being disrespectful for no reason. Prove to me that you don't have the money."

I opened Cash App to send her the $16.00, thinking my bank would decline it because I don't have it to give her. Instead, even with no money, it sent. I gasped in shock as I was sure I was about to get an error message. I got even more angry because that meant I was about to be hit with yet another overdraft fee.

"Thank you, and I'm going to send you some more money anyways," she said and slammed out of the door.

I texted Skyy that I hated her, that she was fucked up for spending money that she never gave me, that I was tired of holding us down while she played in my face, and that she needed to go live with the guy. In hope to scare Skyy and even more hope that she would stop choosing to resolve every disagreement with a physical fight with me, I even told her that I called the police and that they were on the way due to her scratching me while she was tussling trying to get my phone from me. I didn't really call that night, but she did hurt my neck, and I thought more and more about calling after each fight, and this particular night I was very close. Her response was that we would both go to jail that night because I attacked her first, and she will use him as a witness. She left that night and didn't return for a few days.

If I can be a little more honest, I begged Skyy to come back home that night. She responded to none of my texts nor answered my calls.

The next morning, September 13th, I reached out to Skyy again. I explained to her why I was so frustrated and even apologized hoping this would be a conversation starter for us to discuss our problems and move forward, but the only response I got was that she was good, and I should call it quits. She also agreed to move out of the apartment, asked for thirty days but stated that she may be out sooner. A part of me was excited that she finally agreed to move out, and a part of me felt badly we had to get to this agreement the way that we did. She had reasons to feel the way she felt, and so did I. Both of our feelings were valid; although, I felt like my perspective was handled unfairly.

The next day she called, and I just was not ready to talk, so I texted her to give me a moment. She responded that she would still like to discuss the October 1st moving date as she still wanted to live together. I responded that I never canceled the 2 bedroom and that I could use help with the cost of the house moving forward. I reminded her that if I moved forward with signing the new lease, I would be committed to paying it for 12 months.

"So we are officially roommates?" she texted.

"Yes," I responded. To me, this was a way that Skyy and I have always rekindled. To her, she had a hidden agenda.

She proceeded to say, "We need to discuss boundaries."

I told her that I wasn't going to bother, kiss, or touch her. She stated that she wasn't worried about that part and she just wanted to make sure we don't have attitudes towards each other and walk around being disrespectful towards one another because it was unnecessary.

She also added, "Please don't be in my personal business and involved in my personal life. If we decide to be cool, then OK, but if you don't, that's OK, too. I'm not excluding you; there are choices. I just need peace."

To test the energy where she was really coming from I asked, "What if we both decide to fuck every now and then?"

She responded, "No." I then stated that my mind kept changing and explained to her that I really don't like the idea of roommates; she was an exception because she was my partner.

But reader, let's back up to Skyy's request for me not to be involved in her personal business, but in my house? The audacity of this girl to ask me again to continue our cohabitation arrangements but didn't want me involved with her is asinine. Why would she want to keep tabs on me by living together while we are not together but she moves how she wants to move? Also, to slap the word "peace" on that like it was going to sell me the idea was even more insane. How could this be peaceful in a slightly bigger home, and it's not even peaceful in the current home.

I had to tell Skyy no, that we couldn't move forward with this arrangement either because, again, I couldn't wrap my head around it. I told her that she puts me in a hard space when she keeps asking because I really don't like telling her no, but I had to make the best decision for both parties because of how badly our dynamics took a shift. I did ask to be cool and dissolve our relationship on good terms.

Her response was, "No, I'm good. I'll move out today."

I'm so glad I said no because things took another shift that confirmed my intuition was guiding me correctly. I received another text from Skyy that read, "Now I'm in a relationship. I don't mind moving out. I said it'd be cool if we were living together for peace, but now that's out of the picture. I don't want to have shit to do with you, love. I'm good. I'm moving out, and I will never have to worry nor hear from you once I change my number. So I'm happy I didn't decide to be with you. I'll be there today getting my stuff."

Sarcastically, I responded, "Congrats on your third relationship in three months. Hopefully the two of you can be better living partners. Trust me, I'm definitely at more peace than ever, and I will be really good when you move out, and I change my address. I am glad that you two could bond under my roof. I'm not worried. I don't depend on another human for anything. Now, leave nicely before I give you the move out that you really deserve and ask for because I was trying to be nice, but I'm about to show you how girls move their ex-girlfriends out. As soon as I get home on my break, your belongings which are not out of the house will be on the porch. You are crazy if you think you do not have a protection order pending. Your papers will be served to you at Solar's house."

Yes, I was in raging emotions again at this moment. A part of me felt like she was, too, and that most of what she was saying was based on emotions. But on another note, most of me felt like I was right the entire time about Skyy's plotting her life around the benefits of having me in her circle. I never completely felt at peace that she genuinely wanted to be here and this was why. I also had to stop allowing Skyy's inability to control her emotions due to mental issues to excuse her or give her a pass of the actions that followed. Now more than ever I needed to stand on business. Even if it hurt me. And let me tell you, it hurt me!

Since the moment Skyy felt comfortable enough to open up to me, I made and I kept my promise to always be there for her. This sometimes meant that regardless of what transpired between us, I would always be open to reconcile. I never wished for our relationship to get to this point. I felt like a failure. I felt like I was indeed controlling her as she kept saying that I was. I wished that I could have responded better and calmer, but no. This is exactly what Skyy needed.

For years, I've always allowed her to have her way and rest on the fact that I will always be in her corner and if we ever lived together, that I will never separate us but under these conditions I had to learn that all of those promises were being used against me as an act of manipulation. Promises are null and void once a relationship takes such a turn, and for the sake of my healing, or just because, that is OK.

She texted back, "There is no need for you to do a protection order because no one wants you anyways." Around 7:30pm that evening she sent another text stating that I may want to hurry home because she left my door open.

I never headed home to be at home by 8:00pm just in case she was still possibly there. I didn't want to have an encounter with her, so I basically gave her four extra hours without her knowing. I couldn't afford to leave work to check on my house, so I called my cousin to go check on it for me. Within twenty minutes, my cousin arrived and told me the door was unlocked but closed, and the house looked OK. She did say that some things were left on the floor, but there were no major damages to the home, so I continued working and got off of work at my regular scheduled time.

When I arrived back at home a little after midnight, things felt different. I officially had an opp at this point, one who knew literally everything about me, including what time I leave and arrive at home, so I was scared that night and several nights to follow. I opened the door, and Skyy had trashed my fucking house. "Is this the same house that my cousin saw?" I thought. It immediately hit me that my cousin didn't want to alarm me too badly because although trashed, there were no major damages to any of my things, nor was anything of mine missing. I didn't bother addressing with Skyy the condition she left my house in because that would mean more conversation between us, and I could understand she probably felt upset, and that was her way of expressing herself, so I let it go.

As I continued to walk through my house, I noticed Skyy left a lot of her things behind. Three chest drawers were still filled with her clothing, a pair of black Timberland boots were left on the top shelf in the closet, her entire white wooden vanity gifted from Solar years prior and a plastic bag filled with important documents were all still at the house. The very first thing I thought was that she was probably moving so fast, she forgot to double check and look in all of these places to make sure she grabbed everything, or maybe she didn't have enough room to fit any more things in her vehicles or the vehicles that helped her transport her things. The last thing I thought was that Skyy purposely left some things behind because she anticipated another encounter later on, but I feel like that is more of the truth.

There was no way I was allowing that encounter to happen though, not after she disrespected my living space. I texted Skyy that I appreciated her leaving me some clothes and the Timberlands, but the important documents I didn't need.

She texted back, "I'll be there."

Then I politely texted her back, "Oh no you will not." I decided not to stay home that night so I went to my friend's house. This night was the first of many nights in a while that I experienced real peace while sleeping. I didn't have to worry if Skyy was coming home, what time was she coming home, if she came home, how long would she be there before she left home again because our home was no longer her home. I expected this feeling would be what I needed to start healing.

My biggest reason for wanting Skyy and I to separate from the same living space is because I couldn't heal with her still there. She never saw nor cared to see that reason from my perspective, though. What I did not expect and what people who have cohabitated with their partner and later separated don't talk about enough is how hard it feels living in that same house alone. Usually, when Skyy and I went through our breaks, we were already living separately. This time was different. This really felt like the end of Starr and Skyy. I was scared because I did not know how angry she was now and if she may unexpectedly come by the house again. I felt lonely because days prior, this house had more life in it. Our story was never perfect nor did we give ourselves time to create a blueprint for our new dynamics, we just jumped in. From the first day, we officially moved her last set of belongings in feeling so chaotic, I watched our everyday flow become a little more seamless. With just a little more time, just a little more patience and just a little more love, we could have been OK.

All of these thoughts began to crowd my mind at once. I went back and forth with whether I made the right decision. I rested on the fact that I did make the best decision for us.

For a week, things were normal. We shared no communication. I proceeded about my days as I always have while incorporating more time to hang out with myself, friends, and family. I visited the library weekly. Reading and writing helped me tremendously. Memories were still in my head on a regular basis. Sometimes, I smiled at cute and fun memories, sometimes I became angry, and sometimes I cried. I allowed myself the time I needed to feel each emotion. I kept the idea of going to therapy in the front of my mind because I knew that I would need some guidance navigating through all of these emotions.

In an attempt to get myself back out on the scene, I ended up going on a date with a male friend. He and I met up one night a little past midnight for drinks, and after about four lemon drops, I went back home. I had fun with him and would have opted for a second date, but that night, all the tipsiness did was get me in a reminiscing mode about Skyy and how we used to spontaneously go out, lose track of time, and just go to the beat of the vibe.

I texted her at 4:00 am letting her know I was not withholding her from her belongings and that she was more than welcome to come get them if she wanted or storing them at my house was an option as well. I told her to let me know her plans. After two days of no response, I knew I was blocked on her cell. I still had access to direct message her on Instagram, so I sent her a message Saturday morning before I headed out to my hometown, Albany, Georgia. "I texted you." I said.

Later that night when I got back to Atlanta, she responded, "Hopefully about my things and when I can come pick them up."

Then I responded, "Yes, that's exactly what I texted you about." I screenshotted the text thread from the phone showing her the exact message that I sent. We made arrangements for her to come the following weekend. I told her I would wash and organize everything to have in one spot when she arrived. I also asked her to return the spare key to my car, and I asked her if she still had one of my outfits that we shared. I made one special request that if she wanted to keep the outfit, a black crop jogging set, could she bring me some of her oversized t-shirts that I often slept in. The last set of directions I gave were very clear. I asked Skyy to please arrange a time to visit my home when I was either away or to let me know in advance so I can leave the house and allow her to come over without us seeing each other.

Skyy acknowledged her understanding of this simple but very important request. She had only been gone for a week at this point. The pickup date would make it two weeks. I wanted her visit to gather her belongings to be just that. I didn't want us to be forced to be in each other's space on behalf of anything else. If there were a time later on that she or I agreed to meet up to converse, then that would be a separate occasion designed for that. This was not the time. Also, if Skyy were bringing anyone other than Solar to assist her with her things, I definitely did not want to see that.

Something weird happened the next morning. While I was scrolling through Instagram, I received a notification of a recent follow. I click on it. It's Solar! Maybe he's trying to get in touch with Skyy and cannot reach her, I thought. I remember times where I considered reaching out to him to get in touch with her previously, but I never did, so I could understand why he would reach out to me concerning her. To me, something must have been wrong because Solar has never tried to add me on Instagram in three years of knowing me. Also there was a time when we had each other's numbers.

One night, Skyy and I were out, and I got too intoxicated to drive, so she used her phone for GPS, and I talked to Solar on our way back to their house on my phone. I never saved his number or used it outside of that one time. So I hit him up through Instagram messages.

"Is everything ok?" I asked.

"Everything is good," he responded.

So why the fuck are you on my page if apparently you have beef with me. Are you trying to resolve the beef? Do you want some information on Skyy's whereabouts right now because I don't know. She hasn't lived here in a week. All of these are thoughts that I was trying to put together to make sense of why Solar was following me on Instagram. Just in case he told Skyy that I messaged him and it was a problem, I messaged Skyy myself and told her that I did message him on Instagram first because I didn't know why he followed me.

Her response was, "OK."

I dropped it and never tried to see what was up with Solar after that. Since Skyy responded to my message, that meant she was also good. At the time I assumed they were back living together so if she wanted to reach out to him at that point that was between them two.

I proceeded to build up the energy to start the packing process on that morning as well. In a way, having some of her things at the house was a little healing as it allowed me to hold on to some memories a little longer. On the other hand, having her things there felt like things were lingering, and I couldn't fully close the door of that chapter of my life. Box after box, I thoroughly went through every room of the house, every corner and cabinet until everything was neatly stacked by the door. The moment I finished, I bawled. The one thing that allowed us to have some type of communication going between us was about to be gone.

As the week continued, I decided to put everything in the storage outside of my house and leave the storage door unlocked. I realized that my house was starting to feel somewhat peaceful again, and I didn't want Skyy's energy throwing that off, nor did I want to give Skyy another opportunity to destroy the house I cleaned.

She texted the Friday night prior and asked if she could just have ten minutes to get her things out the house Saturday, immediately after work. She did specifically state she would have someone with her to assist her with the vanity. I told her I would not be at the house and that the storage was unlocked that had all of her things. She texted stating that she would be heading to the house around 7am, but by 9am.

After checking the storage, I noticed that she never came over. She asked if we could schedule a time in the afternoon. I told her whatever was easier for her was fine with me. I also told her I would be leaving the house again around 3:30pm, giving her time to coordinate her arrival.

She then stated, "Well, my things are in the storage, so it's cool whenever you leave."

I responded, "Right. So no worries. We will work the schedule out. Get some rest."

Then she said, "No. I'm coming today. Just make sure everything is good in the storage. Please and thanks."

The more I used a cordial tone with her I felt like she was doing the opposite. So I told her, "I know you're coming today, and all of your things are good in the storage. I keep telling you a time because I am not ready to see you. Also, again, if you're bringing anyone other than Solar, I don't want to see them either. You don't have to have the extra hostile tone with me in an already hostile situation. I don't need a reminder of how I contributed to this space we're in because I'm already reminded every day. You're doing well, and I love that for you. I'm trying to make this the very best transition possible by being nice and understanding with the changing schedule."

After that she changed the plans again for the next day which would be October 1st. I jokingly told her to just come back to live there since it was taking her a long time to come grab her things. Next day came, and I thought she would show up and yet again nothing. She was on the way, but I guess something happened. I never asked. I just reminded her that I already said she was welcome to come get them at the best time for her.

She said, "Thank you, love."

I sent a heart emoji, and she sent one in return.

I texted her, "We're still family so don't be a stranger."

She agreed and said we were good.

For two weeks, we didn't discuss any arrangements for Skyy's items. I knew she would come get them when she wanted them. I would not press the issue because it wasn't one. My life continued as normal. I continued to visit the library. I shopped for a new fall wardrobe. I refreshed my hair and nails. I attended a friend's and cousin's birthday party, prepared for Tamar Braxton's concert, and even went to the State Fair. The fun life I had even prior to Skyy was making its way back around. More importantly, I wasn't bothering Skyy nor was she bothering me. I had no facts on where she had chosen to live after our separation, only assumptions. In my head, she was living back with Solar.

In a new outfit and with new hair, I posted a picture of myself on Instagram the night of my cousin's party. I went to sleep, and the next morning I logged back on. To my surprise again, Solar had liked my picture. It's a "like," people go around liking pictures all day, so I still didn't put any energy into the like itself. Solar is grown, and if there were something to be said to me, he knows how to talk. In all honesty, I felt like the opp was watching my life. All I knew for sure was that Solar hated me and had been feeling resentful towards me for some time. The more I ignored him, though, the more he reached for my attention.

Not too long after, another notification came through. Solar's name is on the top of my direct message list and in bold; the only thing I see are the actual words, "2 messages." Had it only been one, I would have been able to see a preview of what he was saying. Seeing that there were two made me think that the homeboy had a lot to say. I proceeded to open the message because now I want to know what's really up. There were two kissing face emoji in one message and the other message read "Don't tell Skyy. We're not together anyways."

I automatically changed every assumption I had regarding Solar trying to reach Skyy and something being wrong and began to think either she was messaging me on his account, or they were both plotting against me to set me up. If this was so, then this is super crazy. I no longer felt safe, but I did feel like I needed a little more information on the motive or what they were trying to accomplish.

I knew they both had separate or some joint reasons to be upset with me. With the amount of time that had passed I didn't understand why they were trying to retaliate now. At this point I began to entertain the situation at hand a little more. I responded with the money emoji which meant the only conversation that needs to be exchanged via my direct message are those which are discussing money coming my way.

The response I got back was, "What does that mean? Don't be like that."

"What does that mean? Don't act like she doesn't need to know anything." I know the way Skyy texts, and I would say that the person behind the messages that I had at hand were of a different texting style in how words were abbreviated and spelled. "Whomever this is please stop playing with me. Both of you," I responded.

"This is Solar. Do you want to call me? You have my number. Trust me babe, I will never do anything to harm you." He messaged back.

This particular text made things even more weird. I felt like he was so anxious to really harm me because why else would he say that. I ended up video-calling on Instagram with a male friend in my presence, hoping that the male would scare them off and let them know that I really do have a team behind me if something like this were to ever occur. But on the video all I could see was a dark screen and the person never said a word. I sent another message saying I would be filing a real police report if I found out it was Skyy, and I advised Solar to speak up for her if it's not her.

The next day, something that alone wouldn't have been weird happened but made this situation even more weird because they were both happening at the same time. Skyy texted me around 7am. "Can I ask you something, or are you automatically going to say no," she sent.

I read her text and didn't respond because I felt like things were beginning to come to the light. I just wanted to watch things play out. Skyy definitely can't keep up with two different messages, I thought. Around 3pm she texted again, "I guess you have me blocked."

I asked her what was up? She asked to use my Door Dash account and I told her yes. We ended up talking on the phone to discuss details and even that conversation seemed normal and unrelated to Solar's messages. It's like she didn't know. The next day I ended up telling her not to use my Door Dash account because "I had something under investigation, and my location was being used," I told her. I was seeing if she would mention anything but she never did.

For days, this wrecked my brain and I couldn't think of how to get to the bottom of this. In my head, remember, I thought Skyy was involved with this so the last thing I wanted to do was text her letting her know I knew it was her. The more my adrenaline began to rush, the more I started to think of ways to get in touch with Solar. I knew since Solar didn't like me that if I called him, he would tell Skyy, and she would eventually come clean about what she was doing behind his account, if it was even Skyy.

I remembered that I had Solar's address in my phone from previous messages between Skyy and me when we were trying to coordinate a drop off/pick up schedule while we were living together. I texted that address to Solar and told him that I will be calling the job the next day to speak with him. The next morning, I kept my word and called the job. He was not available, so I left a message with the receptionist to have him give me a call back. I received no call back from his work phone nor a response from his cell phone. An entire day passed, and I felt even more stuck because there was no way for me to retrieve his cell phone number from my old call log so long ago.

I went to sleep yet another night with a puzzled mind. I knew that with a sound mind, I would be able to think of something else, another way to help me retrieve his phone number. The next morning, I woke up feeling well rested, but still scared. I searched Solar's Instagram page until I noticed that the entire time he has his business page in his bio. It was only listed, not really linked to his personal page, so that's how I never thought to go to his page, but I used his business page to get his cell phone number. Anxiously, I called the number that was listed and Solar answered the phone. In no way was he upset or confused about why I was calling.

"Hello?" he said.

"Hi, Solar. It's Starr. I got your number from your business page on Instagram. Is this you messaging me on Instagram." I asked.

"Oh what's up, Starr. Yes, that's me." he replied.

"OK. What are you trying to do?" I asked, highly confused at how he doesn't see this entire encounter as weird as fuck.

"I was just trying to,....never mind I will let you and Skyy figure that out. I'm going to stay out of it," he said. "Don't worry about it I won't message you anymore," he added.

"OK. Whatever." I responded and hung up the phone. I wish I couldn't worry about it, but not worrying was impossible because I already believe what I predicted to be happening was true. I felt like he was protecting his and Skyy's plan by not telling me why he was messaging me. I also thought maybe he was trying to sit the both of us down and clear the air. If so, that should not have been hard to say. I got tired of trying to figure it out. I immediately went to my leasing office and gave a 30-day notice to vacate my apartment and started planning to relocate. I had nothing set in place but a final move out date. Luckily, because of how delayed things were at the leasing office, I was not under a lease and was already paying the month-to-month fee, so this would be an easy move.

Right after I signed papers at my leasing office, I paid for a storage space for all of my things. I wanted a real new start. I didn't want anyone to have knowledge of where I was nor have access to my living space. Even though a lot could have transpired in thirty days, not much could happen after I had moved.

I put both Solar and Skyy in a group chat and texted them both to leave me alone and keep me out of their shit. I told them that they were both crazy.

He didn't respond at all, but Skyy responded about an hour late after she woke up. "What?" she texted.

I didn't text back promptly, so she called. "Did you know you added Solar and me in a group chat together?" she asked.

"Yes. I did that on purpose," I told her. "Solar has been messaging me on Instagram this whole week, and when I asked him why, he said, 'I'm going to stay out of it and let you and Skyy figure it out,' so I thought you had something to do with it."

In reality Skyy was totally uninvolved with Solar's messages, and I had thought the entire thing out wrong. She stated that she had not been talking to Solar in some days but also put me on some game regarding his motive. "Solar knows that you're the only person who is allowed around the house, and the only person who the dog won't bark at. He's trying to get back at me by giving you some of that weak ass dick," she stated.

I was so shocked. I never expected Solar to initiate that considering he had verbalized that he hated me, but he also had the opportunity to try the poly relationship and didn't approve.

I was also not interested in being involved with their drama. I sent her screenshots of the messages and she spoke with him. He admitted to her that he wanted to get back at her by talking to me. When she told me, I told her again that I did not want to be pulled into it. I was good. I also slipped up and told her that I was relocating because the conversation shifted to us catching up. My move was supposed to be a surprise to her, so I hated that I slipped up and gave her that information, but she still didn't know where. Later that night, she asked if he and I were still communicating, I said no. That was the last conversation I had with both Skyy and Solar for another week.

I needed help taking down my hair and needed more oil for my hair from Skyy, and as a natural response was so close to reaching out to her, but I didn't. It was important for me that even if it felt uncomfortable and different now that I respect her space after our break up. I didn't want to have to risk her telling me no nor did I want her feeling like she had to say yes. This would also mean that we would be seeing each other and sharing the same space, and I still wasn't sure that I was ready for that.

On the night of Tamar's concert, I left work early, and on my way home, Skyy texted me again if she could come get her things the next day as she wanted to get them before I moved. I called her since I was driving. I told her yes and that I was thinking about reaching out to her for her to make me some oil for my hair. She agreed to make and sell me some, and we ended up catching up on how things had been for the both of us.

I told her that I was doing well and that I had been spending a lot of my free time writing and creating, that I was looking to start therapy soon, and that I was getting ready to go to a concert. I also told her that I had perfected her French toast recipe and that I've been eating French toast every morning. She told me she was good as well and that she had not had any French toast since the last time I made her some.

We danced around the idea of her possibly coming over to the house for breakfast the next day or my helping her with a few Door Dash orders.

After about an hour talking on the phone, I had this feeling of ambivalence. The vast of my emotions were warm and happy to not only have talked to Skyy but that we were on cordial terms. In a sense, her voice soothed me, gave me the idea that we were going to be OK. I was so anxious about how conversations between us would be, if any. Even if they took a shift, this was a great start. A little bit of my emotions were still upset at how things transpired between us, though.

I felt like my healing was regressing the more I enjoyed talking to Skyy. I didn't believe that she deserved any soft energy from me. I wished that I could have paused time in this moment for both of us, for this moment to never end, but responsibilities called on both ends, and we both had to go.

While at the concert, I imagined her being there with me. In the moment, I started to reminisce and start planning our entire future out again in my head. After the concert, I texted her to see if she wanted to do some late night orders together. She stated that she had a lot of drama going on that night. I told her to keep the drama where she was.

The next day she mentioned completing some orders but never did. I hinted at her coming by my house to pick me up and she said that was not agreed upon. We didn't talk the remainder of the day until about noon the following night. She used the Door Dash account and was reaching out to me regarding the account when she needed to. I asked her again about my hair, but I could tell she had no plans to do so. I went to the grocery store and came back home to cook. My phone rang, and this was the first time I had the volume on high while she called, so her special ringtone came on. My heart fluttered and I was taken to a familiar soft space yet again.

"Hello," I answered in a raspy tone because I'm trying to conceal my emotions.

"Hi. Are you at home?" she asked.

"Yes, I'm here." I responded.

"I was thinking, since I'm close to your house, if I can come and get my things?" she asked again.

"Yes that's cool," I told her. Calmness abruptly left my body. I got so anxious I could barely think straight. I knew that seeing Skyy, although it may have felt good temporarily, was not the best thing to do in the long run. As much as I wanted to contain my emotions, I wasn't confident that I could take on that strong role when I saw her. Would I react out of anger? Would I act sad around her? Would I be too vulnerable? Bitter? I didn't know. But would a conversation, some time together and a hug feel magical right now? It absolutely would. Besides, when it came to rules, Skyy and I never played by them. We could be broken up and still allow the vibes to flow as they desired. This was normal for us, but we have also proven that our normal was not the best thing for us.

I would like to add that I assumed that Skyy was coming to the house alone. She never mentioned anyone else on the phone, and we had been talking for a few days by now. If there were someone with her, I was sure that she would have remembered my request and respected it since we were in a good space.

Because these were my assumptions, I decided not to leave the house. Instead, I would stay in case she needed help or wanted to talk and spend time. She arrived at the house about twenty minutes later and asked me to open the gate. I got even more nervous. I opened the gate and headed to look out the window. I knew this was wrong because of how uneasy I felt. These were not butterflies. This was my intuition communicating with me, warning me, steering me in the right direction as it always has, never leading me wrong. And this was me turning a blind eye and becoming deaf to it all. I took the risk, gave my heart the lead in this one, and failed myself.

She knocked on the door. I hesitated, but not too long before I opened the door. We made eye contact, and I felt that without saying a word she could tell by the look I gave her that she had me exactly where she wanted me. She handed me the spare key to my car and asked where her things were all while smiling and using a friendly tone. I pointed to the storage and noticed another person coming up the stairs. She brought the new guy to my house while I was present and arranged it so I was forced to see him. They were in matching pajamas! There was no hiding my emotions because my face said it all. Skyy set up the play, and won.

The amount of satisfaction my look alone gave her was all that she needed to thrive. Thrive in the fact that she left me and now had a one up. Thrive in the fact that no matter what request I made, she would violate my boundaries, and there would be nothing I could do about it. Thrive in the fact that just like she had planned, I would suffer. She promised me the holidays and we had planned to do the whole matching pajamas, photos, and family time for Christmas. Matching outfits were our signature go-to since we've known each other, so she wanted to prove to me that my spot had fully been replaced.

I couldn't even stay at the house knowing they were outside in the storage. I walked out of the house, got in my car and sped off with no plans or direction of where I would go. I just needed some time to pass while she finished what she needed to do so I could come back home. She had activated demon time within myself.

My goal now was to make her eat her words and show her life without me or me as her enemy. I texted her telling her that I blocked her on everything, changed the Door Dash logins, and took the money she made on my account. I didn't understand why she had him and was still using resources from me.

She acted like she didn't know why I was upset. "Why are you mad at me? I told you I was coming to get my things, and you said yes. That's really fucked up of you if you took the money I worked for," she responded.

She continued to try to log in to the account but could not get in. She even attempted to get into my email. We argued the entire night until I finally went to sleep. I didn't sleep well that night. I felt that Skyy was beginning to act a bit out of the norm, and I knew Solar would be the only person to understand and can give honest insight on what he thought as well. I didn't know any of the new people she had been hanging out with well enough. Hell, they didn't even know her well enough. Solar and I have been the only two people I have known to know Skyy the most. If anything ever happened involving her, we would be the two to step, regardless of the situation.

Now on the contrary, I also viewed Solar as my final wild card. He would be the card I played to win it all. See, if this whole thing was a game to Skyy, and she played her cards how she chose to this entire time and won, then I would change up from playing with my heart this round. I would play solely for my satisfaction, my enjoyment, and my revenge. I understood and was OK with the fact that if I played this card, there would be no more UNO nights together, now or in the future. I didn't care. I wanted her to feel a fraction of what I felt, and I wanted to see her feel it like she saw me feel it. When I played with my heart, I lost everything. I was numb, so now I felt nothing.

On Solar's behalf, for me it would prove that he wanted the arrangement long ago, and he fumbled by not giving it a try when the opportunity was presented. It would mean that I knew what I was talking about the entire time, and my thoughts and feelings were not from a place of delusions. He would also have his lick back with Skyy.

For me, I would be able to say I had them both and that each time I distanced myself, one of them came back to me. This would be an opportunity to procreate. As long as my ovaries allowed, I wanted to conceive and carry naturally. If I were going to step back on the straight side of the fence, I must make it count. No contraceptives and within my ovulation window would be the only way I engaged. He was spoken for ... a good father, no STDs, and hadn't been with anyone outside of

Skyy. I knew his temperament and personality so I didn't have to go through the process of getting to know anyone new. He and I literally went through the same exact thing with the same exact girl at the same exact time, so there was some type of emotional understanding there. I would do him this solid, and in return, he and I would be cool and have a mutual understanding.

I could feel Skyy's presence on him, so it was my way of not having to detach from her so fast. They had been together so long, they acted alike in many ways. We both still really loved her, even though for me there would be no future with her. They still had a shared responsibility to keep them in each other's lives. Lastly, it's still an arrangement within the original triangle. Even though the triangle never became official, we didn't deviate too far on what the arrangement would have looked like.

I portrayed a humble role, but I was the x factor in the equation. I remembered every dime, every minute, every sacrifice, every tear, every appetite, and every ounce of sleep that I lost during this three year on and off cycle and I took my power back. I didn't let a moral, a loyalty or a conscience get in my way. This was my mission, and I was going to fulfill it. I couldn't help but replay the scene where we were at my house, and she played K. Michelle's "Cry" loudly on the Bluetooth speaker, danced around the house, and looked me dead in the eyes. That was my first time ever hearing that song, so at the time, I didn't know that Skyy was giving me the playbook with my next play already written. She would have never imagined this next card played the way I'm about to play it.

I went back to Solar's direct message thread on Instagram and asked him for a civil, adult conversation. He accepted, and I told him I would call him when I got a moment. He invited me over to talk face-to-face. I told him that I would probably come over the weekend because of the work week and the late hours when I get off of work. He ended up sending me another message stating I could still come over after work since he was usually still awake that time of night. I mentioned it being too cold to get back out after work. He responded that he wouldn't have me standing outside in the cold anyways. It was so clear of his intentions. He didn't care about this damn conversation.

My mind was already made up that I was going to give in to his offering because that was my lick back, but this conversation was just as important to me because there was some cloudy air that needed to be cleared first. I had heard from Skyy that Solar called me out of my name, said he hated me, and talked a lot of shit about me. I believe he said everything that was repeated to me, and I wanted him to know I knew his true feelings towards me. I wanted to clear my name and let him know that I never took his girl from him. Whatever issues they had prior to me were unresolved, and she and I both willingly allowed us to get as far as we did. In the beginning, I could admit to stepping over his toes with my demands for Skyy's attention, but the more I got to know them both and accept the situation at hand, I gained respect for him. What I could never apologize for to him nor her was that I truly loved her. That was something I couldn't control.

I took a shower, headed to the liquor store and let Solar know I was on my way over. I grabbed him a shot of Hennessy and myself a shot of Casamigos. If I were going to move forward with this, I had to gather and place myself in a less normal headspace. I arrived at his home, and he let me in. I immediately handed him his shot of Hennessy, and I chased my Casamigos with juice. He handed me a joint, and we started talking.

He asked me what had been up. I told him I was just trying to rebuild my life back after Skyy. I explained how our last encounter transpired and told him that I was worried about Skyy. He reassured me that Skyy was OK and that she was just living her life now and technically wasn't doing anything wrong. She just wanted her freedom for a change. Then I shifted the conversation towards clearing the air. "So what's your beef with me because I never took your girl from you," I asked him.

He played it off and said he never had beef with me, and he didn't feel like I took his girl from him.

"Well you did say you hated me," I said.

He admitted to saying it but said it was just out of anger.

I didn't like how this conversation was going. He wasn't being truthful and accountable for his actions towards the situation, and I know he felt a way about me for some time. I stopped digging for information and clarity regarding the past and allowed myself to go under the influence. We continued to converse.

"When do you want kids?" he asked.

"Now," I responded. I told him about how I enjoyed my 20s and that in my 30s I wanted to bring new life into the world, nurture, and love them.

He joked about me having twins, but I told him I would be fine with that. His asking didn't bother me at all. In fact, we had already had this conversation before with Skyy and Solar's mom present. Although I do feel a little invasive every time someone brings up my fertility, I understand that it has become the normal subject matter to converse about for some people. In Solar's case now, it was an important question and the grown-up thing to ask.

"So what are you trying to do and why now?" I asked him.

"I mean, I always thought you were sexy," he said.

I gave him this look that said shut the fuck up, because I'm not going to say he never showed it, but when it mattered, he never showed it enough. I reminded him that he was the one to disapprove of the arrangement the second time it was presented because it was I who disapproved of it the first time.

He asked if I really thought we could have all worked out. I told him yes. The love was there, the respect grew on us and there was no competition between parties. Financially, we would have all been in a better situation as well, keeping finances under one roof. When our energies naturally flowed and everyone was comfortable in their own lane, everything moved in harmony. She had her love with him and she and I had our love and chemistry amongst us. The few times this happened, I would sit back and just admire what a unique situation we had. The vibe always got interrupted by egos and misunderstandings.

He told me that he didn't think it would have worked because they hadn't been on good terms for a long time and that they just continued to play the role. I remembered she had told me that, too; I just didn't know when they were on, off, or just playing the role.

"Roll another joint," I told him. I couldn't risk that shit wearing off anytime soon.

"That liquor starting to hit?" he asked me. He was checking the vibe.

"Hell, yeah," I told him." "

"Are you going to lie down before you get on the road?" he asked again.

"Yes, I'm about to crash on the sofa for a little while then head out." I was the right amount of tipsy where I was feeling really good but not sick. I had just enough courage and carelessness to not give a fuck and do what I needed to do. I was glad that things were starting to move a little swifter because I was ready.

"You can come lie down in the bed. I'm not going to bother you," he said and chuckled.

I followed him into the bedroom. I remembered the bed in his room being so comfortable from when Skyy and I slept in there together. I asked for some shorts as I began to unbutton my pants. He handed me a pair and I changed from my jeans and laid down. I was depending on him to continue suggesting the next move. Obviously, I was down to agree.

"You want to cuddle before you go to sleep?"

By now I'm not even talking, I'm just doing everything he suggests. It was my way of mentally role playing with him. We never cuddled though. I went straight to straddling across him and laying on his chest.

He held me, and I started kissing his lips. Now skin to skin, I performed an act that he did back, and from there he dedicated his undivided attention to the needs of my body. He explored and pleasured places in me that I had never been introduced to. Solar took his time with me and made me the leading Starr of the night. I never liked a journey that was too fast, too rough, or just outright selfish. He would be sure to meet me right where I was with what I liked, switching to brake or accelerating the gas pedal when appropriate. Sharing roles of dominance and submissiveness, I whispered affirmations in his ear. Like a gentleman, he followed the "ladies first" rule, but he didn't follow suit after. There wasn't a release of replicated DNA from him to me.

My plan to leave his house and go home to go to sleep was crushed by his desire to cuddle. Now this makes me uncomfortable. Our cuddle chemistry was incompatible. I was the five-minute touch, roll over and go-to-sleeper, and he was the eight-hour macro touch, when you move, I move just like that sleeper. I could feel just by the way he slept under me that he probably missed Skyy, regardless of what he said. I could resonate with that, so I allowed him to play out his fantasy to its entirety. I let him hold me and give me unwanted body heat while we slept.

I woke up around 5am to head home. He got up and I jokingly told him that I didn't see that he left any money on the nightstand for me. Definitely in a sober state of mind, I thought on the way home, but not too much. I enjoyed my night with Solar and wanted to go at least a day not talking to him just to show him a clear visual of what this dynamic was. We really had nothing else to talk about until I wanted to meet up again, if I wanted to meet up again.

I was supposed to text him when I made it home but I fell back to sleep. He texted me to check in, and I told him I had made it home. Around noon he called me, but I didn't answer. He proceeded to text me. His energy became hard to ignore. After not responding for about 2 more hours I texted him back when I got to work. I tried to tell him

I was a bad texter and that was the reason for the delay, but he didn't believe me.

He told me," I know I didn't just get used for all my goods all for you to disappear now." That's exactly what this was but since he called me out on it, I denied that being my motive. Even with Solar, no matter how hard I tried to be, I considered his feelings, too, and shifted my attitude when I felt like it was too hard. There's no hiding it; I'm truly a soft girl.

I went to work and close to my departure time, he texted me asking if I was coming back over after work. I told him that I didn't know because it felt dangerous, and I felt like I was betraying her. I wished circumstances were different, meaning I meant Skyy was included. I told Solar that I had a lot to think about. He responded that it felt good and asked me why I felt like I was betraying Skyy if she has moved on from the both of us? I asked him what if I got pregnant and told him to delete our text thread.

"And, sir, you didn't pay your invoice," I texted mid-conversation, laughing. He said that he got me and tried to convince me that I may as well come back tonight to cuddle because he knew I didn't want to sleep alone, and neither did he. I lied and told him that I had to work overtime until 3am. I just wasn't ready to do this the next night. Per my Flo app I was still ovulating and I was approaching my most fertile day so I considered that as well.

The ovulation took the lead and two nights later, I was back in Solar's graces and embraces. I was at my most fertile this night, so my energy was a bit more aggressive. My body had a high demand for some good pressure. I showed up to the job ready. Solar, on the other hand, late? Absent? No, present but not performing! I was pissed. I didn't know that I had approved time off. My tone got firmer with Solar, but even that didn't help shift the mood that night. He blamed it on being too nervous. I smacked my teeth, rolled over, and closed my eyes. I couldn't help but calculate the amount of time that had to pass by for me to get back to the same part of my cycle for this opportunity to present itself again. Now I understood Skyy's frustration. Her sex drive was extremely high, so I could see how the inconsistency had her feeling. My soul wanted to hug her and tell her it all made sense now, but that wasn't possible. I started to miss her again. It dawned on me that she was my natural reaction to a lot of things, and not having her around anymore really meant that I would be doing life without her. I got a clearer picture for what that looked like.

I gave Solar a pass and for an entire month, we continued to see each other about three times a week. Sometimes he would come over to my apartment, sometimes I would go to his house. I always set a 5am alarm to go back home, and that just became normal.

My communication got a little more consistent with Solar. Sometimes we talked on the phone for hours; sometimes we texted back and forth for hours. We talked about more than sex. We planned to hang out together, we talked about the workday, we made commentary on how good our most recent intercourse was compared to the previous one. We talked about fantasies and created a sex bucket list together. On that list, we added a threesome with a girl of my choice because Solar had no one to add. We also added ocean-view balcony sex where we would be required to go out of town in order to check that off. I included a threesome with Skyy as the biggest task on the bucket list. I told him I didn't know when nor how, but I felt like it was still in the cards for us. I went as far as reaching out to whom I thought would be the perfect girl for our threesome, and she agreed to vibe with us. He told me he liked how I controlled the arrangement and got straight to the point when I showed him the text thread of my sealing the deal.

We were becoming more comfortable with one another. He wanted to turn me out, and I let him. We tried new things in the bedroom, but he never reverted from spots that were guaranteed to satisfy me each time. I noticed Solar began to release a lot and often. His releases were external, but I know that method to be only so effective. Either way, this never worried me. My cycle comes to visit but only lasts two days versus a week. I considered my recent move, my new sex life, and stress and emotional levels. I never felt that I had received what I needed to be planted to have a worry of anything else.

Then, I started to feel my appetite change. For me, even this is normal. Sometimes I eat a lot; sometimes I don't. Sometimes a certain food bothers me; sometimes it doesn't. Nausea came and left, but I tied it to PMS. I didn't think too much into it as I would wait to see what happened the following month. So I continued enjoying my time with Solar, and only Solar.

Some mornings, I would snooze my 5am alarm at Solar's house and extend it to 6am. Some mornings, he would stall my leaving and I had to remind him of why it was important that we continue to be proactive in our schedule. I knew at some point, Skyy would find out. If I could prolong that encounter, I would. We would discuss the what ifs for when it did happen, but neither of us never knew what the reaction would be. I began to think about starting to park my car away from Solar's house or even mentioning to him about clearing his garage for me to park in it, just in case Skyy ever rolled by. At least she wouldn't see my car first. I never made it around to discussing this with Solar, though.

After Thanksgiving, I came back to Atlanta from visiting my family, and Solar and I had been too far from each other too long. I went to his house that night with a plate I had brought back for him, and the ride to his house on this particular night felt different. Two people had called me, and I had told both of them I was headed home or to the store when they asked me where I was heading in the car so late. Solar also told me that the twins had not fallen asleep as quickly as he planned. I had also been driving the entire day and should have just crashed at my new place, but instead I took the hour drive to Solar's house.

When I arrived at his house I still didn't mention my parking in the garage, although it was on my mind. He let me in the house and the entire house was awake. There were no signs of anyone being asleep anytime soon. While we waited around, Solar's phone rang, and I saw Skyy's name on his screen. He hurried and answered the phone and they conversed with her on speaker. I was tuned in listening out to see if I could hear car background noise or waiting to see if she would be coming to the house soon. That feeling came back again. That loud intuition feeling. I should have called this night off and waited another night.

Solar asked Skyy if she were coming to the house, and she said no. That was probably enough for him, but not for me; I couldn't be so sure. She had also mentioned to him that he was supposed to FaceTime her earlier that day and never did. I thought that would have been a good time for me to leave, but they never switched to FaceTime.

Probably because this night moved so differently, I forgot to set my 5:00 am alarm. Once we did get settled in around 2am, we went to the bedroom, and Solar showed me how much extra you get when you return home from out of town. The way he was welcoming me back made me want to go out of town again! I fell asleep and slept so good, too good. Around 6:00 am Solar was trying for another round, but I couldn't.

Not too long after I had rejected Solar, the dog came into the room growling, alarming us that something was going on. Solar woke up and checked outside and came back to the room. His demeanor, though, wasn't calm.

"Is she here?" I asked.

"I think so," he responded.

I got up and rushed to put my clothes back on. I found everything except my sock, but Solar didn't bother to help me find it. He left the room again for a better view, perhaps, and indeed, she was there, attempting to enter the house through the window.

I heard him talking to her. "Really Skyy? So you're going to break into my house?" he asked in an amplified manner.

I reached under his pillow and looked at his phone to see if I had missed something, and there was no text nor missed calls on his screen. It was time for me to face it, face her, and deal with it. My moment was here. Now it was time to give Skyy the "my turn" look while she looked at me in shock, hurt, and disappointment. I did it. I got something past her that she never saw coming, something that if nothing else could, definitely got her attention. Most of all I did something that she had been wanting to do with me for a long time and she had no control over it getting done.

By the time I made it to the front door, she had made it there before me. He was standing in front of her to keep her from going any further. From a distance, I looked at her from head to toe. I first noticed her hair was freshly done and her wicks had grown out. I had a quick moment to gaze at her sexy, angry face; then we met eyes. That was the million-dollar moment for me. From the look in her eyes, I knew if she could have gotten to me at that moment, she would have not spared my life one bit. The last thing I noticed was a box cutter in her left hand. I reached for my purse and keys, and Solar reached for Skyy.

"Her tires are slashed!" Skyy said.

She continued to wrestle with Solar. He was able to get the box cutter out of her hands but was not able to keep her away from me. She grabbed me and started hitting me in the face, pushing me into the couch, and got on top of me. My legs were the only thing free so I kicked her in the face with one UGG boot on.

"If you slashed my tires, I'm calling the police on you," I told her.

"You will be the one going to jail for trespassing, so call them," she said back.

She was probably right. Once the police responded to the call, someone was going to jail. I couldn't leave the house without tires on my car, and her license did have the address on it; mine did not. Even with proof that I was an invited guest and she broke in through the window, I wasn't certain that the police would see it that way. I didn't want to risk a record over this, so I thought about it. I was able to push her back off of me until she fell on the floor, and Solar made an attempt to get her again. She got back to me, ripped my shirt, and opened the door. She threw my other UGG boot outside along with Solar's keys and pushed me outside. I went to my car, and she had slashed two of my tires. I called 911, and this time I stayed on the phone longer than I ever have in the past with her.

"911. What's the location of your emergency?" the operator answered.

My mind was taken back to various scenes where I wished I had moved forward with calling on her. I froze up, maybe even snapped back into reality, and hung up. The reality was that even with the situation at hand, I was angry, and I did want to hold Skyy accountable for my tires, but I didn't want to see her or myself being arrested over this. She was scorned, and I contributed to that, so it wouldn't be fair nor smart for me to have called the police.

Solar did come to my car to check on me. I told him that I just needed to get home because I felt sick. I asked him about a plan for my tires, and he didn't have one. I instantly got even more aggravated with Solar at his lack of concern and urgency about my tires.

"Don't worry about your tires. I can change your tires," he kept telling me. I had to worry because I only had one spare in my trunk so there was still one tire unaccounted for. It also seemed to me like he was moving in slow motion. I needed him to already have been working on the tires. Since he didn't, I had to call a friend who would come take the tires off of my car, take me to the tire shop, purchase two brand new tires for me, and take me to breakfast after my eventful morning.

Solar was more focused on the fact that another male was coming to help me. He was mad. I had to do what I had to do. I was clearly alone in this situation. The more I waited, I felt even more sick. I kept feeling nauseated. It wasn't until this moment that I started to consider my recent body changes for more than what they were. I realized that this is not what I wanted with Solar. After this day, I wanted nothing to do with him. He showed me that he really doesn't have control over his own life, and in adversity, he couldn't stand the test. Maybe I was looking forward to Solar owning his actions as I have owned mine. I probably was looking for him to help us reconcile. I really don't know what I expected, but whatever he showed me was not it. I began to worry that I could possibly have a shared responsibility with Solar that will force us to stay in each other's life beyond this day. I prayed that this wasn't so. Even though I did believe that I was clear, I wanted to be very sure. Because I wasn't happy about this possibly being what I thought, I knew that he was not the person I wanted that moment with, nor did I want to be attached to Skyy longer than I had to.

I drove to Walgreens and purchased the most expensive three-pack early detection kit that I could find, as if the more I invested in the test, the more the results would work in my favor. Reading no instructions prior, I ruined the first test. After waiting the longest, most antagonizing five minutes of my life, I celebrated that negative test result in pure joy. A few hours later Solar texted me to check on me and out of anger, I cussed him out.

The next day I spoke to both of them on the phone. Skyy was still extremely upset. Solar was explaining that he never took a side and he tried to break the fight up. I started to tell him how I no longer wanted to see each other and how I took a pregnancy test.

Before I could get my words out he interrupted me saying, "You know I never nutted in you, Starr."

I told him that I believed that to be true but for peace of mind, I wanted to take a test for myself. His reaction made me even more upset, and I saw him in a different light. Knowing that I have not been with another male in two years and I chose him made me disappointed in myself. Days passed, and I was reminded to forgive myself and move on. I still had to get my thoughts across to Skyy. I had logic behind everything I did; it doesn't make my actions right, but I still wanted to explain myself. The email would explain how I went numb after she and I separated and I continued to hurt her because I felt like she was hurting me.

10 A Glimpse in reverse

Sometimes I wish I could go back and make some different plays. I knew the toxicity and the passion wasn't enough to sustain our relationship and that someday our twin flame would be extinguished. I prolonged this process as long as I could for my own comfort. I always hoped for our break up to be cordial, but I knew that was probably farfetched. Lust has its way of making one blind and leaving one vulnerable. I do believe love was present in the mix, but so was lust. I'm often asked if I still love Skyy. Most of the time, my answer is all over the place. The most accurate expression of my feelings towards that question is that love doesn't diminish overnight. It doesn't develop instantaneously; neither can it go away in that manner. For me, it's one of the last things to leave. Even after distance has been practiced, boundaries have been created, and conversations ceased, some of the love still lingers. I don't have to show it in the same way that I am used to showing it, but it's there.

There will always be memories to commemorate special moments. I will continue to smile and shine light for moments that have uplifted me. I look at my past as a necessary experience to mold my future. I don't wish to erase or forget anything that I have survived. When tears come, I allow the tears to flow as they provide me with a cleansing release.

I wasn't innocent. I played a role in rushing something to fit my timeline when I should have healed and worked on myself. I knowingly walked into our relationship with insecurities and voids that I depended on someone else to fill. That's a lot of expectation to put on someone. I did a lot of reacting and thinking with my emotions, another thing hurt people do. I also made a lot of justifications when I continued to accept and exhibit toxic behaviors that never changed. I received some insight that forgiveness can be an inhibitor for continued behaviors. When I was shown I was going to be forgiven for the things that I did, I felt comfortable to repeat those behaviors.

My love for me, however, surpasses all. I owe it to the scars on my wrist and shoulder for constantly reminding me why to not double back. I learned that anything good that came from no sacrifice usually doesn't end up being good for me. I am working to become more intentional about the life that I want. Another wise woman once shared a gem with me to take time to observe people's intentions. "When you are blessed with things, especially things of materialistic value, people can be more attracted to those values rather than the value of your love and character," she told me.

A few times throughout this chapter of my life, I found myself questioning the reasons behind all of Skyy's returns into my life. As my journey progresses, I will embody patience when faced with the yearning desire to share my life with a romantic interest.

As far as my healing, it's continuous. I haven't fully decided to welcome a mental health professional right now. For the most part, I know how to tap into my inner self and find the better version of myself within. I've found that being present for myself to be the most effective method. If I don't let myself down, it will be hard for anyone else to do so. I started putting actions towards my verbalized goals to make sure everything I want to happen, happens. When I see pretty flowers, I buy them, take them home to arrange them, and just look at their beauty. When I discern chaotic energies that are in opposition to my peace, I dismiss them from my space. My vibe is a privilege to experience! I am working hard to make my name a household name, and I will not allow anyone with impure intentions to connect themselves to anything I have going on for myself.

On a quest to reconnect with me again, I am embracing my hair in a natural state, aiming to continue the journey for a full year. Another person will never have the power to strip me of something they believe I embrace the most, and something they feel that makes me beautiful.

I will fully love myself without the comfort of added enhancements when it comes to my hair and embrace the beauty my hair has to offer me, naturally and authentically.

I am finding that the openness for genuine people rather than the search for a specific person is a better journey for me. I consider myself a "butterfly," a free-spirited being, so I don't need a label to establish an understanding. I see labels as a way of boxing me in or conforming me into something that I don't fit in. Labels are set to satisfy the understanding of someone else's perspective of me. I know who I am, so I never put a label on myself. When people refer to the rainbow LGBTQ and try to assign me to a letter, I simply tell them that I identify as the "B," but not for Bi-, for butterfly. One day the wind may place me in the face of someone who is not female. I trust that what is for me will be for me and that I will receive it at the perfect time. My love starts in the mirror! This is my journey, my story, my way! I will know that I have fully fulfilled my mission and my purpose once the transparency about my experiences helps another person.

about the author

LaKymbria Rhodes is a native of Albany, GA. She obtained her Bachelor of Science in Healthcare Management at Clayton State University and has been pursuing her career in Healthcare Finance for 8 years. In 2017, LaKymbria competed in the Miss Georgia USA Pageant. With some accomplishments checked off her list, there was one dream left unreached. Since childhood LaKymbria has enjoyed creative writing and reciting poetry. Last year she returned to the performance stage with her first original erotic poetry piece and promised herself a published book by age 30. As a birthday present to herself, *Toxic Passion* was released Feb. 18, 2024!

www.ingramcontent.com/pod-product-compliance
Lightning Source LLC
Chambersburg PA
CBHW022143020726
47496CB00008B/2536